# UNION LOCAL TRASHES
# SPACE COLONY!

A long shot of space colony Don Quixote appeared on the screen. Both cylinders were off center, pulling toward each other, and cutting into the mirror array.

A puff of gas shot along the window-bay seam and the cylinder slowly began to bend. The window bays, which had been dark and clear, turned white. The depressurized cylinder now swung slowly into the intact cylinder, tearing a gap a hundred meters wide. There was another puff of gas, and the other cylinder started to disintegrate. Bright flashes showed that this time glass was being thrown around.

There was an arterial spurt of water from the severed aqueducts. The close-up shot showed the mundito in the process of disintegration. Beside it, the long-range shot showed a small, twisted structure with a brilliant white tail, blazing in the sunlight, and growing visibly longer as they watched.

"That will show up on Earth as a tiny, transient comet," said Skaskash, "but from here the view is utterly spectacular."

# The Revolution from Rosinante

Alexis A. Gilliland

A Del Rey Book

BALLANTINE BOOKS • NEW YORK

This book is dedicated
to Dolly, with love.

A Del Rey Book
Published by Ballantine Books

Library of Congress Catalog Card Number: 80-68219

ISBN 0-345-29265-0

Manufactured in the United States of America

First Edition: March 1981

Cover art by Chris Barbieri

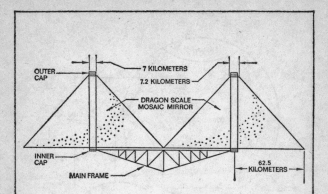

OUTER CAP

7 KILOMETERS

7.2 KILOMETERS

DRAGON SCALE MOSAIC MIRROR

INNER CAP

MAIN FRAME

62.5 KILOMETERS

**FIGURE 1: a. Mundito Rosinante assembly**

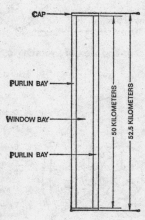

CAP

PURLIN BAY

WINDOW BAY

PURLIN BAY

50 KILOMETERS

52.5 KILOMETERS

**b. Vertical cross-section of a rotating cylinder**

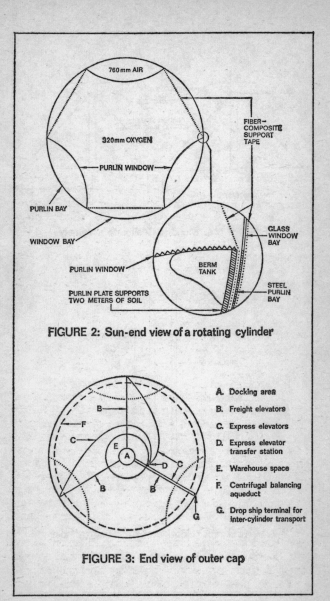

760 mm AIR

320 mm OXYGEN

PURLIN WINDOW

PURLIN BAY

WINDOW BAY

FIBER-COMPOSITE SUPPORT TAPE

GLASS WINDOW BAY

PURLIN WINDOW

BERM TANK

STEEL PURLIN BAY

PURLIN PLATE SUPPORTS TWO METERS OF SOIL

FIGURE 2: Sun-end view of a rotating cylinder

A. Docking area

B. Freight elevators

C. Express elevators

D. Express elevator transfer station

E. Warehouse space

F. Centrifugal balancing aqueduct

G. Drop ship terminal for inter-cylinder transport

FIGURE 3: End view of outer cap

# CHAPTER 1

Charles Chavez Cantrell sat in the rear of the Stateside Café drinking black coffee and writing on a yellow pad. Change orders positively demanded a handcrafted answer, and here were two, arriving within hours of each other. The one from Mitsui might possibly have merit. The one from Scadiwa, the Southern California Agricultural Desalinated Water Authority, was an obvious loser. Scadiwa must have been trying to get Mitsui to sign off on it until Mitsui had an order they needed Scadiwa to sign. He sipped his coffee and studied his draft memo.

From: Gyfox, Rosinante Div.
Subject: Change Order, Proposed 4/14/39
To: Scadiwa, ATTN: Sr. Manuel Jorge Panoblanco

Dear Manuel:

Par. 1. Medium flowery expressions of esteem.

Par. 2. Regarding your proposal to substitute the "classical, well-proven aluminum/mylar mirror" for the dichroic layered mirror presently specified, I regret to inform you that you have used the wrong numbers to develop your cost estimates. Asteroid Rosinante moves in an elliptical orbit, 1.32 AU at perihelion to 3.85 AU at aphelion. This is not the same as moving in a circular orbit at 2.58 AU.

Par. 3. The projected savings for such a change are correct for the unit area of mirror, but, unfortunately, Gyfox has already leased the mirror-making machines for the anticipated duration of the job. Whether we use the machines or not we are obligated to pay rent on them. Happily, production is running right on schedule.

Par. 4. Let me explain the layered mirror to you,

Manuel. When one alternates layers of high and low refractive materials, and makes these layers exactly one-half a wavelength thick, a stack of layers seven or eight deep will reflect that wavelength, say red, while transmitting all other colors like clear glass, so that you have a dichroic mirror reflecting red only. The layered mirror we are preparing for Mundito Rosinante is a composite, red, green, and blue layers stacked on top of each other, so that the reflected light appears to be white. We do not reflect infrared or ultraviolet, so that the light is much cooler than raw sunlight.

Par. 5. Ah, Manuel, I can hear that estimable old lady, your bookkeeper, saying: "What does he need such an expensive mirror for? Buy him a cheap mirror just as good!" The reason for using the layered mirror is this: Our mirror shines less heat into the mundito, so that we need less heat radiated out. That is the job of the primary radiators, which have already been built, and which were designed to handle the load from the layered mirror, not from an aluminum/mylar mirror of the same size.

Par. 6. If your bookkeeper remains unconvinced, Manuel, please feel free to send her here for a visit. I would be honored and pleased to show her the work we are doing here.

Par. 7. Warmest regards to your family, and my profoundest gratification at your continued understanding and support.

> Effusively,
> C. Chavez Cantrell
> Project Manager

After reflection, he scratched out "seven or eight deep." No need to boggle management's tiny minds with details. The robot waiter refilled his cup while he studied the Mitsui change order. Mitsui had far better engineers than Scadiwa, but the change was still troublesome. It would add considerable strength at a nominal weight increase, but it would be very difficult to execute. He was wondering whether to temporize and ask Mitsui what sort of catastrophe they were anticipating, when the president and the treasurer of the union walked up to his table.

"May we join you?" asked the president, as they sat down.

"You just have, Don. What's on your collective minds?"

"Scrambled eggs and home fries," said the treasurer.

"Oh, hush up, Lucy, we have a grievance."

Cantrell looked around. The first shift was beginning to come in for breakfast, and the place would soon be jammed.

"Why don't we go over to my office and discuss the matter, then?" he suggested. He paid his bill and they went down the hall to the project manager's office, a small cluttered room whose only pretense to luxury was genuine oak parquet flooring.

"You won't find any higher or more responsive management within a day's walk," said Cantrell affably, settling into his high-backed leather chair. "What seems to be your problem?"

"Well, you just posted the schedule for glazing the bays, and the crews are going out in suits instead of switching to remote control," said the president. "The contract says we go on remotes three years after a sunspot minimum, and we want remotes, that's all."

"Well, now, Dornbrock, do you suppose that was three years after the minimum began, or three years after it ends?" Cantrell asked.

"Crap on that stuff, Charlie! The contract says it's time for remotes, and that's the way it's going to be."

"Hey, Don . . . we haven't had a sunspot for thirty-seven months, not one. This is the sunspot minimum, right now." Cantrell leaned forward in his chair. "You don't *need* remotes, right."

"Don't GIVE me that stuff, Charlie!" yelled Dornbrock. He hit the desk with his fist, and a pile of papers slid off onto the floor. Lucy picked them up and handed them to Cantrell.

"Look, Dornbrock, why the hell do you think the contract calls for remotes, anyway?"

"Because of the radiation hazard, Charlie," said Dornbrock with exaggerated patience.

"That's right. The clinic has that gene reader, so union parents won't have defective kids," added Lucy.

"Right. The contract also specifies a radiation level at which remotes will be used, regardless of the day or date, doesn't it?"

Dornbrock sat scowling, his arms folded, but Lucy nodded. "That's true," she said.

"Right, Don?" prodded Cantrell. The president nodded grudgingly. "Okay, then, you aren't worried about sun-spots, you're worried about radiation. Forget about the sunspots. We don't have them. It doesn't matter. How is the radiation level?" There was a rather long silence.

"Low," conceded Lucy at last. "It's way on the safe side."

"All right, Dornbrock," Cantrell said, "stop letting that little contract analyzer do your thinking for you. You take this to arbitration, you got to believe management is going to win."

"Yeah, Charlie, maybe so," said Dornbrock at last. He stood up. "Come on, Lucy, let's get some breakfast." At the door he turned back.

"You still ought to go on remotes, Charlie," he said.

"Peace, Don," replied Cantrell. After they left he looked again at the Mitsui change order. Presently he dialed his computer.

"Aren't *we* early this morning," it said sweetly. "And what can I do for you?"

"You have the Mitsui change order, honey?"

"Of course."

"Fine. I want a quick and dirty comparison between the Mitsui purlin window and the specified purlin window when you detonate a fifty-kiloton device near the center of the mundito."

"Quick and dirty, eh?" said the computer. "Well, in both cases the window bays will lose twenty to thirty percent of their total glazing. The specified purlin window nearest the blast will deform along the short axis seams and lose maybe point two to point five percent of total glazing . . . a few hundred hectares. The other two purlin windows appear to be deformed along the short axis seams, and would probably be leaking." There was a short pause. "The Mitsui purlin windows are not deformed, and seem not to have lost any glazing. Not even the one closest to the blast."

"Well," said Cantrell, "and maybe double well as well. That seems to answer my question, now, doesn't it." The computer, recognizing a rhetorical question when it heard one, was silent.

# CHAPTER 2

On the second Tuesday in November, 2038, the electorate of the sovereign state of Texas voted on Proposition 4: To build a low-cost housing development in San Antonio, on the site of the Alamo.

The argument over Proposition 4 dominated the election, and in the end it was passed by a few thousand votes after a quarter of a million votes were challenged and rejected.

Luis Raoul Panoblanco, the incumbent governor of Texas, and the chief architect of Proposition 4, was reelected by 87 votes. At the time, it was widely believed that *all* the rejected ballots voted against him. It was subsequently established, however, that the figure was only 98.15 percent.

In April, Governor Panoblanco ordered the demolition of the Alamo so that construction could begin. It was simply bad luck that he made his announcement immediately before the spring break. Nobody could have foreseen that Anglo college students from all over Texas would descend on San Antonio seeking to impede the march of progress.

Captain José Menendez of the Texas State Police sat in his mobile command post and smiled at the television crews.

"One final question," said the interviewer. "We have just learned that a number, perhaps more than half, of the state troopers who performed so gallantly this afternoon have called in sick this evening, and may not be in tomorrow. Would you care to comment, sir?"

Menendez looked properly stern for the cameras. "Yes. Those men are Anglos, and I understand that, but they are also Texas State Troopers. Governor Panoblanco has been informed, and he has invoked his emergency powers to dismiss any officer calling in sick without proper cause. As you know, several of our men are in the hospital, and . . . what is it, Tomas?"

"The name is Riley," said the officer. He walked over to Menendez' desk and set down a box full of badges in front of him. "Tommy Riley, ma'am," he told the interviewer, "formerly of the Texas State Police." He removed his own badge and tossed it into the box with a musical clink. "And I ain't never going to help no fucking greaseball tear down the Alamo."

"We'll be back after this word from our sponsor," said the interviewer, smiling toothily.

When the Texas National Guard arrived the next morning, the construction machinery the state police had been defending was burnt-out scrap iron, and the Stars and Bars flew over the Alamo.

In the governor's mansion in Austin, Governor Luis Raoul Panoblanco conferred with his aides and allies.

"Jesus X. Christ!" he shouted. "Why am I served by incompetents?"

"You didn't want anybody around smarter than you, Luis," said State Senator B. J. Coya coldly. "The Anglos in the House are moving for impeachment, and we can't keep the Senate out of session after Easter. Now what?"

"Make them stop! You control the committees! I must have time to work out of this!" Panoblanco paced back and forth, running his hands through his hair.

"Time isn't going to help," said Coya. "Promising amnesty to the people in the Alamo, and then arresting the ones who came out for felonious assault and destruction of property was—forgive me, Luis—an unforgivably stupid thing to do. And on statewide TV, too."

"Statewide TV! Jesus X. Christ, B. J., why didn't the statewide TV bleep that Tommy Riley statement? To hell with television!"

"The censor must have been Anglo," said one of the aides, "but they shouldn't rebroadcast it as the ad for impeachment, I think."

"The Ad Hoc Committee to Impeach Panoblanco is paying plenty to run those ads," said Senator Coya. "Why shouldn't the TV broadcast them?"

"Slander and defamation of character!" yelled the governor. "I'll sue the bastards!"

"A suit has been filed," began another aide, when a National Guard general entered in full battle dress.

"We are ready to storm the Alamo with segregated units, Governor," he said. "One detail requires your personal decision." He brought the clipboard under his arm to the ready position. "What disposition is to be made of the surviving defenders?"

"You're going to storm the Alamo?" Coya looked shocked and alarmed. "Merciful God," he said.

"We must move fast and decisively!" said Governor Panoblanco, displaying resolution and firmness. The general looked properly impressed.

"Scadiwa returning your call, sir," called a secretary in the next room.

"I'll take it at once!" snapped Panoblanco. "General, I'll be with you very shortly." And he bounced into the next room to take his call.

"Scadiwa?" said the General. "Isn't that in California? What is he talking to them for?"

"His brother Manuel is the head of Scadiwa," replied Coya. "The only explanation for the time they spend on the phone is a conspiracy to conquer the Universe. Would you like a beer?"

"I would be pleased to drink with you, Senator Coya." They walked over to the bar. "Carta Blanca," said the general.

"I believe it's time to switch to a local brand," said B. J. Coya. "Give me a Pearl, *por favor*."

# CHAPTER 3

From the May issue of *The Skeptical Economist*, Arthur Feuerstein's column.

The failure of the Geneva meeting of the Proud Tower consortium to agree on the allocation of cost has ended the chance to start construction on the orbital lift in this decade and probably the next as well.

The excuse offered in the final communique, the current business slowdown, is utterly pathetic. The prospect of spending that much money on the orbital lift would have brightened the economic outlook immensely, even though cash outlays would not have begun before the fourth quarter. The real reason is political rather than economic: the North American Union's unwillingness to see its presently dominant position in space eroded by foreign—particularly Japanese—competition.

Whatever the reason, and whatever the long-term consequences, the short-term consequences are serious and potentially disruptive. Ecufiscale Tellurbank has assumed an enormous inventory of mortgages on mundito real estate. Now that the Proud Tower with its promise of easy access to that gold mine in the sky is out of the picture, the Tellurbank has got to figure that it is over-extended. A retrenchment is in order, possibly a major retrenchment, and sooner rather than later. The pain will be felt all through the economy, but particularly by those companies which have invested heavily in munditos, most notably Mitsui. The Japanese Government may be a silent partner in the numerous Mitsui ventures, but without the Proud Tower even the Japanese Government is going to feel the burn. In the next quarter look for foreclosures as these companies cut their losses.

Now would be a good time to check your portfolio and weed out the deep-space stocks and mundito bonds. Both appear far more speculative than they did last week. The smaller companies involved in space-contracting work should also be sold off. Typically they are well run and heavily leveraged, and not set for a protracted bear market. These include the Hannaur Group, CDC/Mars, Demeter Construction, Bannerman and Voss, and Gyfox.

Despite the present limitations on shuttle flights, look for the shuttle stocks to pick up—Boeing, Douglas-Lockheed, Furtwangler, and Mitsubishi. The prospect of building the Proud Tower has kept them depressed, but they now appear to be safe to hold in the near term, and a good buy for short-term speculation.

At the end of a long oval mahogany conference table shone a telecon screen in the slide-projector mode. In the semidarkness of the richly appointed board room, the men who ruled the farflung Mitsui enterprises sought consensus in the timeless Japanese manner.

"The first slide," said a hoarse voice at the other end of the table, "was covertly obtained from Ecufiscale Tellurbank."

"This is authentic, please?" A polite question to affirm what all knew.

"Unquestionably authentic, Admiral Kogo" was the reply. An easy point for consensus. Then the first slide was shown, light-blue type on fluorescent-stained bond.

This is a memorandum to the file. April 14, 2039, at the Executive Dining Lounge in the Ecufiscale Headquarters building, I had lunch with the Vice President for Loans, Col. Ras Mohammed, and our esteemed president, Hsu Ko Jing.

Hsu treated us to a lecture on economic theory, how desirable it would be to lower the creation rate of money by 3–4 percent. Reminded *me* that the eicu is the economic indexed credit unit.

After years and years, Col. M. got approval for hands-on inspection and auditing before we make a loan. Why? Why, if it will slow down the rate of money creation, we ought to give it a try, says Hsu.

We had a little quarrel between the red snapper and the Charlotte Russe, Hsu and I. The very smallest of quarrels, as I urged increasing the loan rates to discourage speculation. Our honorable president prefers to reduce the size of the loans we make, instead. From 10.115 times construction costs to 8 or 9 times, a bruteforce method of the most brutal variety. Col. M., the birdbrain, suggested a compromise: start at 8.5 and move up to 9.0 or 9.1, twitter twitter.

Our esteemed president smiled fatly and said that was an excellent idea, and that I should give it serious consideration. In the event that I agree, he will be *most* happy to put it into effect. And the sooner the better.

We agreed that the NAU shortfall in grain production will be troublesome if grain is bought with eicu. No action.

We agreed that it would be nice if the sunspots came back, to raise the ozone level and thus get the shuttles moving again. No action there, either.

/s/ Isoruku Llamamoto

Admiral Kogo lit a cigar, and drew on it so that it glowed redly in the darkened room.

"This would appear to support my contention that we may be somewhat overbuilt, would it not?" he said politely. There was a subdued agreement. Mitsui knew it was overbuilt, but was reluctant to face the consequences.

"Since we agree that we are overbuilt," continued Admiral Kogo, "it would appear prudent to cut back at this time, would it not?"

"I must agree," said the hoarse voice. "Not only prudent but regrettably necessary."

"Well, then, Mr. Kijin," said the admiral, "since we agree that we must retrench, the question becomes only to what extent, does it not?" The words fell into velvety silence. Nobody wanted to retrench, but nobody could object to retrenchment, either.

"The next slide," said Kijin hoarsely, "shows the degree of completion of twenty-eight active projects. The twelve finished mundos will, of course, be kept. Are we agreed?" There was a polite if uneasy murmur of consensus.

"Agreed," said Admiral Kogo, drawing on his cigar.

"The five in the design stage will be terminated immediately," continued Kijin, "losing architect's fees and a few options." He coughed. "This, also, appears uncontroversial." There was pained silence as several dreams ended with unseemly abruptness, but no dissent. "The eight which we are building by ourselves, will, I am afraid, have to be deferred indefinitely."

"I am terribly sorry, Mr. Kijin," said Admiral Kogo, "but deferral would soon prove more expensive than completing the projects." He blew a ring of smoke that floated slowly across the table. "These projects must be terminated."

"Termination seems rather drastic," said a well-modulated baritone. "Is it truly needed?"

"So sorry, but yes, it is needed," said Kogo.

"I agree," said Kijin, coughing. "Termination is bitter medicine, but medicine Mitsui must take."

"We cannot defer?"

"So sorry, Oyama-san, it is impossible," said Kogo.

"It is unfortunate, Oyama," said Kijin sadly, "but we must concur."

"Agreed," said Oyama. The corners of his mouth turned down, and he sat silently, seeking to master his emotions.

"Thank you so much," said Kijin. "The three remaining projects are about a pair of asteroids orbiting around a common center, Munditos Don Quixote, Sancho Panza, and Rosinante. Each is a joint project with a different NAUGA."

"Oh, shit!" growled Kogo around his cigar. "Speak Japanese."

"Of course, Admiral. NAU Government Agencies—North American Union Government Agencies—joined us in these projects as one means of adjusting our balance of payments at the national level. I seem to recall that we unfortunately agreed to arbitrate any disputes in the World Court—"

"Exactly so," put in Oyama, "and we also conceded that Japanese jurisdiction would not apply. Except, of course, by mutual consent." A titter ran around the room, easing the tension.

"The projects are well along, also," added Kijin, "and it would appear that the penalty clauses for unilaterally withdrawing will equal or exceed the cost of completing the work." He coughed. "I truly believe, Admiral Kogo, that we would be well advised to continue."

"Such a course appears to be prudent," Kogo conceded, tamping out his cigar in the ashtray and replacing it in its glass tube for future reference, "but those projects are marginal. They should not be brought to completion at any cost."

"We will watch costs very closely," promised Oyama, "but for now it is the choice of lesser evils to continue."

"The World Court has lately exhibited a shocking anti-Japanese bias," Admiral Kogo admitted. "I, also, must agree."

"The second item of business," said Kijin, "concerns our automassage line. First slide, please." Admiral Kogo, uninterested, picked up his briefcase and made an unobtrusive exit. "As you see," continued Kijin, "Mitsui has enjoyed excellent success, capturing twenty percent of a rising market. However, in the last quarter we have experienced severe backorder problems. Next slide, please. Here are our choices: Expand the Kyoto plant or build an overseas plant near our major marker, in Shanghai. I recommend building in Shanghai. Yes, Mr. Fujita."

"Would you show us the slide which projects the market shares and estimated building costs, please?"

"I would be delighted," said Kijin, coughing. He reached into a pocket and produced a slide, which he held up. "Here it is. Kyoto should cost less and should give us about the same market share. Nevertheless, I urge we build overseas."

"The balance of payments?" asked Oyama.

"In part," Kijin agreed, "but the main reason is that Mitsui has promised the municipality of Kyoto to hire more Korean workers, when and if we expand the plant in Kyoto."

"Those Koreans *are* Japanese," said Fujita. "They are native-born citizens."

"That is what the mayor of Kyoto said," replied Kijin hoarsely, "but they are *also* Koreans."

"Then it is clear that expanding the Kyoto plant is the rational economic choice, Mr. Kijin," said Fujita politely. "Would you not agree?" When Kijin said nothing, Fujita called for a vote.

Economic rationality lost by a wide margin.

# CHAPTER 4

Mitbestimmung is management and labor playing high stakes poker with a tarot deck. The point is to maximize economic rationality *and* political stability.

Don Dornbrock sat in Cantrell's office, an untasted cup of cold coffee at his elbow, his green silk jacket with "Union President" across the back in red and gold letters hanging on his chair.

"Let's try it again, Charlie. We do one-hundred percent inspection on the window bays and purlin bays, okay?" Cantrell nodded. So far, so good.

"The shift comes off inspection to build those mickey-mouse Mitsui pretzel benders for making those purlin tiles. Shift on shift is double time for each shift, right?" Cantrell nodded and rubbed his eyes.

"Then we pressurize."

"If you say so, Don. But if we pressurize now, we have to build an annealing oven for the purlin tiles, remember."

"Can't be helped. We build the oven on single shift, at time and a half because we get no break."

"Time and a half," Cantrell conceded.

"Okay. We start up the pretzel benders, and pop the tiles into the oven. Two days' dwell time, right? Of course right. We go back onto shift on shift, and now we'll be working in shirt sleeves, not suits. We start the purlin window frames, going flat out. Double time again."

"How far do you figure to get in two days' time, Don?" asked Cantrell.

"At shift on shift? We'll finish the number-one purlin window-base frame, and be aligning the Shelobs to start the number-two frame . . . maybe we spin the first beam on number-two before the first tile pops out of the oven to lay on number-one. Maybe."

"Right. Now the annealed tiles are rolling out of the oven."

"Right! We begin tiling. Shift one tiles, shift two works on the number-two purlin window-base frame, and shift three sleeps. Then shift three goes to tiling, shift one goes to the base frames, and so forth. Double time."

"Hey, Don. What about the number-one purlin window-cover frame?"

"I was coming to that, Charlie. The first pass around, we lay the tiles in the base frames over all three purlins. Then we strike the oven, on single shifts—"

"Forget the oven, Don. It's not in the way. I want the cover frames done."

"We strike the oven on single shifts. It's a break in the rhythm, and a chance to rest up a bit."

Cantrell nodded agreement. "Time and a half because of no break," he added.

"It's a pleasure to do business with you, Charlie," Dornbrock said, grinning. "*Then* we build the cover frames, on double shifts again—"

"At double time, again."

"Oh, hell, yes. Then inspect and pressurize the purlins."

"It'll have to be one-hundred percent inspection again, Don."

"That's a pain in the ass, but okay." Dornbrock picked up a plexiglass model of the purlin tile, two tetrahedrons joined at one edge to form a flat, diamond-shaped surface with incised dimensions of 354 by 408 centimeters. He pressed the catch, and it unfolded into eight hinged triangles, which lay flat and straight, a piece of tape cut at a sixty-degree angle at each end. "Clever, these Japs," said Dornbrock.

"Okay, honey," Cantrell told his computer, "let's have the printout of the contract modification." The computer disgorged a densely printed piece of paper, which Cantrell initialed and handed to Dornbrock.

"God. Six-point type, and no margins," muttered the union president. He placed the paper on the scanner for the union's contract analyzer, and when the light flashed green, he also initialed it.

"Now we sell it to the members," he sighed. "Mitbestimmung is hell."

"Look on the bright side," offered Cantrell. "All that overtime will cause management such pain. . . ."

"Maybe. Maybe not. You're management, Charlie. Do *you* care that we're into a lot of overtime?"

"No. You'll be busting your collective humps for it. What cares me is the job gets done."

"Right. Do you think those jokers at Mitsui give a damn . . . 'what cares me'? punchy, punchy, Charlie."

"*Es posible*, Don." Cantrell picked up the strip of eight triangles and folded it back into a diamond-shaped tile, closing with a soft snap. "I gave Mitsui a cost estimate, and they said do it. They never see the work, only numbers and reports. I'm the last man who actually has a hand on the job; from me on up it's nothing but clowns playing with numbers to make money. For Scadiwa, Mundito Rosinante is nothing but the logo for a bond issue."

"Won't Scadiwa and Mitsui share the facilities here?" Dornbrock asked.

"That's the agreement. Scadiwa has so many slots, and Mitsui has so many. You can bet that Scadiwa is going to sell those slots to *somebody* . . ." Cantrell stretched and yawned. "Wouf! Scadiwa is speculating, build cheap and sell dear. I'm going to bed."

"Fair enough," said Dornbrock. "It's been a long day." He zipped up his green president's jacket and walked out into the empty corridor.

In the center processing the prisoners taken at the Alamo, Captain José Menendez poured the last of the light, sweet coffee out of his thermos and fingered the bristly black growth of beard beginning to show on his chin.

"That fool of a governor," he said sadly. "One of his aides just called to tell me not to treat the prisoners so gently. Emiliano, the Anglos are going to impeach his ass for sure, this time, and he wants me to be rough on the prisoners."

"Wasn't he trying to fire you the other day?" asked his lieutenant.

"*Sí*. As if *I* had made the Tommy Riley statement. He could not fire me, so he had to back off, but did he apologize for what he said? No! All he said was his temper is what put him in such a fix. What could I do? I smile and say how I understand, the imbecile."

"He is still the governor," agreed Emiliano.

"*Es verdad.* And I am still a captain in the State Police of Texas, so I am responsible for processing the prisoners here, I think." Menendez took a sip of his coffee. "As I tell my people, it is to be done professionally, not like those pigs in the National Guard. Christ, what a mess they made!"

"I heard they killed thirteen people," said Emiliano.

"Fourteen, counting the sergeant shot in the back by his own men. And two more have died in the hospital, and more than two hundred wounded." The captain's phone rang, and he picked it up.

"Captain Menendez here." He looked at Emiliano and rolled his eyes upward. "Lieutenant, the governor wants to know how many we have done, and how many we have to do, and how soon we will be finished. *Pronto!*" Emiliano looked at the running tally the computer was keeping, and wrote the numbers on a scrap of paper, which he handed to the captain. "Sir! at three fifty-eight AM we done 2,316, and 172 remain. We should finish by four forty-five, no later than five AM." There was a long pause. "Yes, sir. I shall await your orders, sir." Menendez made a sour face at the phone and hung up.

"What did he want?" asked Emiliano.

"We are to finish at four forty-five sharp. No slipups! There will be transportation for the prisoners, and I am to be corvée officer. My orders weel—will arrive on the telefax in a few minutes."

"Hey, Captain," said Emiliano, "the matron has some business." He reached out and switched the picture to the large monitor screen. They watched a young woman with shoulder-length blonde hair walk hesitantly into the processing room as the matron put down the magazine she had been reading, and stood up.

"Hello, honey. I'm Officer Johnson. Let me take your jacket, thank you. And your shoes." The girl hesitated, then removed her shoes, wedgies with urethane foam soles, and handed them over.

"That's a good girl, honey. Now the rest of your clothes, please."

"Officer Johnson is very polite. That is good," observed Menendez.

"What for?" asked the girl.

"We have orders to strip search all prisoners, honey," said the matron. "That's not just you, its everybody."

"I don't want to strip," said the girl, shaking her head. "I won't strip!"

"I'm not minded to argue, honey," the matron replied. "Just lean up against that wall, then." The girl leaned against the wall, reluctantly. "Hands further apart, honey. That's fine. Now back your feet away from the wall. More. More. That's fine, honey." The matron carefully patted down each leg, then undid the macrame belt and felt around the waistband. "Pull in your tummy, honey," she said, unsnapping the jeans and unzipping the fly. "That's a good girl. Now hop your feet together." When the girl obeyed, Officer Johnson yanked jeans and panties down below the knees, exposing tan legs and the white shadow of a bathing suit.

"Hey!" the girl protested. "What is this!"

The matron calmly unbuttoned the blouse up the back. "Why, honey," she said, "you *got* to be searched. Some officers would have told you to do it, or they'd have the men in to help. That's not nice, to make a poor girl do something she don't want." The unbuttoned blouse was pushed over the girl's arms, and the matron undid the strapless bra and removed it. "Now just work your feet out of them pants. There's one, and there's the other one. Real good, honey." Officer Johnson picked up the jeans and panties, and held first one arm and then the other to take the frilly white blouse. She spread the clothes out on a wheeled table, and pushed it through a curtained door to be fluoroscoped.

"Okay, honey, spread your feet again. Beautiful." The matron applied a little lubricating jelly to her fingers, and moving gently and without haste began to explore the vaginal opening for contraband.

"You old bitch, you're enjoying this!" exclaimed the girl.

"There's no law says you can't enjoy your work, honey." The clothes cart came back through the curtain. "You're clean, honey. One thing more and you can put your clothes back on." Officer Johnson walked over to the clothes cart and picked up a slender plastic tube about 20 centimeters long. She unscrewed one end and slid out a flexible yellow object.

"Now this may feel a little strange, honey, but it won't hurt a bit." With one hand the matron spread the girl's cheeks, and with the other she pressed the yellow object against the anus. The yellow object bulged, and began to ripple, and gradually began to work its way into the colon.

"This is what we call a Tapeworm Tranquilizer," explained the matron. "It works its way into the large intestine and attaches itself to the wall. It measures tranquilizer into your bloodstream to keep you calmed down. It measures two or three things in your blood so it knows whether to raise or lower the dose, and when it runs out, it lets go, and you just flush it down the toilet without ever knowing it's gone."

"That's great," said the girl shakily. "Did the others get one too?"

"Oh, yes, of course. Everybody got one. For a couple of days you may feel a bit woozy until the dose stabilizes, then you won't worry about a thing for a few weeks." The yellow object vanished from sight. "That's it, honey," said the matron. "You can get dressed now."

Menendez turned off the monitor.

"That Officer Johnson is very good," he said, "I wish we had more like her."

"When did we start using the worm?" asked Emiliano, knowing Menendez had recently given a course on the subject.

"In the early nineties" was the reply. "The idea was to have a naloxone dispenser for junkies, like the insulin dispenser for diabetics, to provide the dosage as the body needs it." Emiliano grunted assent and sat back to watch the girl dressing on the small monitor.

"The problem was to put the thing where the junkie couldn't get at it," said Menendez, looking at his audience to make eye contact. "But I see it is not very interesting for you." He reached over and turned off the monitor. The telefax beeped and issued a communique.

"Must be the governor's orders," said Menendez, snatching the paper.

"So," he said. "I am to deliver the prisoners to Señor Chavez Cantrell at a place called Rosinante. All meals and transportation arranged. Embarkation point is from the roof of the main hospital here, at five hundred hours on a chartered air ship." He stroked his stubble thoughtfully. "Best I have an officer pick up my shaving kit from home."

"Have your wife pack a change of socks," suggested Emiliano. "You may be gone longer than you think."

# CHAPTER 5

The exalted rank of Colonel Ras Mohammed, Vice President of Loans for the Tellurbank, was clearly marked by his office, which had a bed but no desk, and was furnished in what Dr. Llamamoto had described as Moorish whorehouse.

Now he sat with his senior analyst and long-time aide, Dr. Marian Yashon, in beautiful but uncomfortable chairs at an elaborately inlaid coffee table, supporting an ornate and richly gleaming coffee urn of such magnificence that it seemed only proper that they should be drinking from styrofoam cups the secretary had brought in a cardboard box.

Dr. Yashon was an Israeli woman in her early fifties, short, rather heavy, with gray hair cut close and severely tailored clothes. She had provided the drive and intellectual coherence that raised the energetic, charming but rather undisciplined Colonel Mohammed far above his level of competence.

"Believe me, Marian," he said, "I am terribly sorry to lose you, but President Hsu insisted you were the best person for the job."

"I've advocated hands-on inspection for years, Ras," she replied, "but this is not the way we conceptualized it. Certainly I never thought *I* would be the inspector."

"This is purely to give you firsthand experience, the hands-on experience. When you come back, you can write the first handbook, and none of your field people can say: 'You don't know what it's like,' because you were there. You understand?"

"I understand, Ras. I never worry about what my subordinates might say to me, though."

"You are a hard woman," said Colonel Mohammed with

a faint smile, "but believe me, this way is the best. Have you selected your team?"

"I have," she said. "You will miss their services if not their obsequious flattery."

"You didn't take Odarchenko as I recommended?"

"No! The man is a courtier. I can't use a courtier in the field. Besides, I dislike the son of a bitch!"

"You can't let your dislikes govern your actions, Marian. I want you to take him!"

"He isn't going, by God!"

"Don't be stubborn, Marian!"

"Odarchenko and I cut a deal, Ras. I took Corporate Skaskash and Odarchenko stays home."

"What?"

"Odarchenko didn't want to go, so he signed over his ten percent of Skaskash, Inc. instead."

Colonel Mohammed looked annoyed. "Odarchenko doesn't own the outstanding shares of Corporate Skaskash. The Econometrics Institute of Kiev owns them."

"*Did* own them," corrected Marian. "Title was transferred to one S. A. Odarchenko shortly after Kiev beat out the Rockefeller Institute for our big study contract."

She handed him the stock certificate.

"It seems to be in order," agreed Colonel Mohammed. "I wish you had consulted me about this beforehand, though."

"I wish you had consulted me about this whole business beforehand, Ras."

"Yes, of course. But it was what President Hsu wanted."

"I understand, Colonel Mohammed." The formal address was a mild reproach. Colonel Mohammed had a tendency to brown nose.

He looked at his watch and stood up. "Well. You still have a couple of hours before you have to leave to catch the Laputa shuttle. Will Skaskash be going with you?"

"Now that I have the outstanding ten percent of Skaskash, Inc.? You'd better believe it. The rest of the team will be up as soon as their orders are cut."

"Excellent, Marian. Why don't we go down to the little farewell party your friends are throwing for you? I sprung for the caviar—a half kilo of prime Caspian beluga."

Admiral Kogo settled down into a black leather chair and lit a fresh cigar. The windows in Kinjuro Kijin's office gave a breathtaking view of Tokyo and the bay, and he drew on his cigar and savored the beauty of the panorama before him.

"Forty years ago," said Kijin in his hoarse voice, "my father brought me to meet his superior officer for some reason or other. I looked out these same windows, and the air was so fouled with smog that you couldn't see the shoreline of the bay."

"I remember," replied Kogo. "At the Imperial Naval Academy we kept our white uniforms for special functions, and wore khaki for regular dress. The whites wouldn't stay clean in the ambient air for more than an hour or so."

"Yes," agreed Kijin, "and then the oil ran out. So sorry, no more oil. But Japan survived, and now the air is clean. But you perhaps wish to discuss a problem more current. *Ne?*"

"Ah, so, Honorable Kijin," said the admiral, "it is true. A strange thing has happened with the Mitsui-Scadiwa project at Rosinante. The governor of Texas has illegally sent a shuttle into orbit. This shuttle is illegally transporting twenty-five hundred prisoners—political prisoners—taken at the Alamo. Students, mostly. White, male, English speaking, about twenty, to judge from the newscasts. In orbit they have been transferred to *The Star of Mexicali*, bound for Mundito Rosinante with a cargo of rubber trees."

"They have filled Scadiwa's slots with political prisoners?" exclaimed Kijin. "How remarkable. Why did Scadiwa permit this?"

The admiral blew a smoke ring. "The governor of Texas is Luis Raoul Panoblanco. One of my aides reviewed Scadiwa's T/O and highlighted all the Panoblancos, and Panoblanco in-laws, and Panoblanco cousins. There are quite a lot of them.

"My guess is that someone at Scadiwa may have instigated the move. The governor will get the blame for tearing up the ozone layer with that unauthorized shuttle flight, but that has to be the least of his worries. Meanwhile, Scadiwa has staffed up the mundito, and after taking the loan from Ecufiscale they will immediately default on it."

"You don't think the governor cares that the shuttle flight was destroying the ozone layer?" asked Kijin.

"No" was the confident reply. "He only cares about

bringing down as many of his enemies as he is able. He is mad to punish his enemies while he still can."

"I see," said Kijin hoarsely. "You think he is going to be impeached?"

"Unless he is assassinated first," Kogo replied. "Texas politics are very strange. The Alamo prisoners, however, are up and cannot come back down. They will arrive at Rosinante in forty-two days' time, and that is where they will stay, because there is no other place that will have them."

"Ecufiscale won't make the loan to Scadiwa," said Kijin, coughing. "Not when the mundito has been staffed with young men of military age, even if they appear to be plausible civilians. With that staffing on the Scadiwa side of Mundito Rosinante, Ecufiscale won't give us a loan on our side because of long-term political instability. Hell, we might not be able to get loans on the projects at Don Quixote and Sancho Panza."

Admiral Kogo drew on his cigar and smiled. "I quite agree, Kijin-san," he replied affably. "It is utterly clear that the best and safest policy is to cut our losses at once, and cancel all three projects. Those other NAUGAs, as you call them, with whom we are building Sancho Panza and Don Quixote will, in the circumstances, surely agree to terminate, and we can argue that Scadiwa has unilaterally breached its contract with *us*, and go to the World Court seeking damages from *them*."

"Ah so," said Kijin sadly, "would you like some tea, Kogo-san? Shizu!" he shouted. "The tea cart, please!"

Governor Luis Raoul Panoblanco sat at his desk in the governor's mansion, the flags of Texas and the North American Union at his back to frame the picture, the Great Seal of the State of Texas above his head on the wall behind him. Two of his bodyguards stood by the television crew, watching alertly for a false move on the part of cameras that had already been searched and searched again. Outside the office, more bodyguards watched exits and entrances with great vigilance.

At nine minutes, thirty-two seconds into his scheduled half-hour speech, he was saying:

". . . and the proof that God is on my side is that on the very morning of the day that I banished the Alamo mutineers into orbit, a sunspot appeared! The first sunspot in more than three years appeared in my hour of need! God has stretched out his hand to me!"

At eight minutes, fifty-five seconds into its scheduled flight, a cruise missile, stolen from the NAU Air Force, whistled down the street, bobbed over the fence surrounding the governor's mansion, rolled to miss a large oak tree, and crashed through the window and drawn drapes of the governor's office at 650 klicks per hour to explode a metric ton of high explosive where the governor's desk would have stood if it hadn't been moved to the other side of the room to accommodate the television crews.

In the event, the fact that the governor had moved his desk did him no more good than the fact that he was wearing the best bulletproof vest on the market. The place of honor at his funeral was occupied by a hamburger patty of governor, bodyguards, and television crew.

# CHAPTER 6

The berm tank runs along the seam between purlin window and purlin plate, the full length of the purlin. Roughly triangular in cross section, it rises in height to thirty meters above the floor.

Taking advantage of a mildly ambiguous report of flawed welding, Cantrell slipped away from his desk to revel in the work firsthand. He was standing in a cherry picker near the top of the seamside wall, trying to extract his little finger from a hole along the edge of the weld. "You say this hole repeats in a regular line, Sam?"

The crew chief looked up at him. "Yeah, boss. Along that same weld, one per plate. Thirty-six holes in all. You think we maybe have to reweld?"

"No." The finger came out of the hole, minus some skin. "The weld is sound. What this looks like is a dent on the stacked plates. Something hit the stack, and when the plates were set out for welding, they each had a little ding in about the same place. What you want to do, Sam, is drill out a hole, thread it, and screw in a bolt. The five-millimeter plate will take thread real nice."

"Okay, boss" came the reply. "I'll put Willy on it right away."

Cantrell's belt phone rang. "Tell him I want it done this shift." He snapped open the phone. "Cantrell speaking."

"You have a call from *The Star of Mexicali*," said his robot secretary, "Captain José Menendez on the line."

"Isn't Dario Yzquerida the captain?" asked Cantrell.

"At last report," agreed the computer. "Will you take the call?"

"*Buenos días,* Captain Menendez," Cantrell said. "What can I do for you?" There was a brief pause as light conveyed the message over some distance.

"Have I the honor of addressing Señor C. Chavez Cantrell, please?" Again the pause.

Cantrell sucked on his wounded finger. "Yes."

"Señor Cantrell, Captain Yzquerdia says *The Star of Mexicali* is routed on to Mars after it stops here, and will not return to Earth for many years. Is it not possible to return to Earth from Rosinante?"

"Transportation is often available at Rosinante," Cantrell said. "Are you in a hurry?"

"Sir," blurted Menendez, "I am a captain of the Texas State Police, and when the prisoners have been delivered, I would very much like to go home!"

"If you please, Captain, what prisoners are you talking about?"

"I am the corvée officer for the Alamo mutineers," Menendez replied. "Surely you have been advised of their arrival."

"Surely I have *not*, Captain! *The Star of Mexicali* arrives in three days' time with a cargo of rubber trees, and that is all, so far as I know." Cantrell paused for a moment. "Corvée implies a rather large number, Captain. How many prisoners are you delivering?" There was a pause rather longer than the normal time lag.

"There are 2,491 altogether, including 62 women" was the reply. "You have truly made no preparation to receive them?"

"No." For a moment, Cantrell considered jumping out of the cherry picker. Then he decided against it. With gravity only revved up to about 300 cm/sec$^2$, he might merely break a leg. No sense in taking chances. "As it happens, Captain Menendez, it has been your honor to break this truly astounding piece of news to me. When you arrive, we will seek to arrange your expeditious passage home." Menendez started to say something, and Cantrell cut him off. "Please excuse me, Captain, I'm terribly busy right now." Cantrell snapped the phone shut and took the cherry picker down.

"Say, boss," Sam said, "since we started putting spin on, it's going to take longer to fix them holes. It's not like it was when you could float along the ceiling from one to another, you know."

Cantrell looked at his crew chief and unshipped his motorbike from the back of the service vehicle. "That's your problem," he said. "I want those holes fixed this shift."

He kicked over the motor, and went putt-putting off down the berm tank.

Sam shrugged. "I'll put Fast Eddie on the other end," he decided.


Lucy Schultze stuck her head into Cantrell's office. "You wanted to see the union, Charlie?"

He looked up from one of the computer displays. "Hi, Lucy. Pull up a chair. Isn't Dornbrock coming?"

"Don is tied up in the steward's meeting," she said. "He and Brogan are playing Robert's Rules of Order."

"Can you talk for the union?"

"Don asked me to see what you wanted. Is it about those Texican revolutionaries on board *The Star of Mexicali*, perhaps?"

"Word does get around," Cantrell agreed.

"Fine. The union will work shift on shift to fix up their housing under the emergency clauses in the contract."

"That won't be necessary, and that wasn't what I wanted to see you people about," he said. "We're retrofitting the cassette magazine as a transient barracks, and the plans and work schedules should be out for the first shift." He gave her several pages of hard copy. "This is what we're doing."

"That's pretty crude," said Lucy. "Portable toilets?"

"It'll do for the week or so they'll be in there."

"I don't see any air-conditioning," Lucy said. "Twenty-five hundred bodies will generate a lot of heat."

"We bring in cassettes filled with ice cubes, and replace them when the ice melts," said Cantrell. "Sort of a portable heat sink."

"And no shielding?"

"The magazine is hung behind Asteroid Rosinante on the south polar boom, Lucy. That takes care of the solar radiation. For the time they're going to be there, the galactic background radiation isn't a problem."

"So why did you want to talk to the union, Charlie? This is mostly shirt-sleeve work, and not much of that."

"The problem is, we have to feed them," he replied. "Housing isn't the problem, but it will take time to grow food. I'd like the union to share food with these people until we get a bigger harvest in."

"What do you mean by 'sharing,' Charlie? They eat it and we don't?"

"What the hell do you think sharing is? Cut ten percent off your diet—you eat too much anyway."

"Sure, Charlie. *I* wouldn't mind sharing food. I'm trying to lose weight. But the union? I don't think they'd go for it, I really don't."

"Will you ask them?"

"Sure, I'll pass the word along, but the answer is going to be no. I just know it. What are you going to do then?"

"I've already ordered the standby methanol converter put into operation. We can process methanol into single-cell protein faster than we can make methanol, and I suppose we can step up duckweed production, but that gives those kids a diet of maybe eight or nine hundred calories a day."

"For how long?"

"How long does it take to go from egg to fried chicken? They won't be eating regular until we get the wheat and soybean harvest in from purlin one."

"They'll live," said Lucy uneasily. "The union might go along with some overtime so you can get them fed faster, but they won't share."

"What about drawing down existing stocks?"

"That's inventory management, Charlie. As long as we get fed, nobody is going to look at what you do in the warehouse, but put us on short rations, you'll get struck sure as hell."

"Is that you or the union, Lucy?"

"Charlie, that is my reading of how the union will react. Once it gets put to a vote, it's shot down. And you can bet the stewards are going to be counting calories for a while, too."

"Okay," said Cantrell. "Management isn't going on short rations, either."

"You'll be hearing from Dornbrock on this, I expect," Lucy said as she went out the door, "but I doubt it will be any different."

When she had gone, Cantrell called the head of the commissary department.

"The union isn't going to fuss about drawing down on existing stocks," he said with a smile.

"Well, in that case, we don't have any problem, boss. I imagine they didn't consider livestock as existing stock, though."

"I expect not, Harvey. By the time they discover they're eating lower on the food chain we should be well on our way to rebuilding the herds with vegetable biomass from purlin one."

# CHAPTER 7

Date: May 2, 2039
From: H. Oyama
Subject: Termination of Mitsui/NAUGA projects on
Don Quixote, Sancho Panza, and Rosinante
To: K. Kijin

This office has evaluated Admiral Kogo's proposal to terminate the subject projects. His reasons appear sufficiently cogent to warrant a careful review of our options, but immediate termination of all three projects may be premature.

An alternate strategy which commends itself is to utilize Mitsui's places on Rosinante for marriageable females without other qualifications. This will satisfy Ecufiscale that the large number of single males on Rosinante are not a cleverly disguised military force. Since sunspots have reappeared, it will be a very short time before the ozone level is sufficiently restored to permit resumption of regularly scheduled flights. It is suggested that the wedding flight be placed in readiness to launch at the moment that the ozone level touches the acceptable mark. There will probably be a number of similar flights, and failure to be among them may cause costly delays.

Once we have restored the sexual ratio on Rosinante, it is probable that Ecufiscale will automatically approve the loan. In this event we can reconsider Rosinante's utility in terms of whether or not it is sufficient to repay the loan. This will assure a satisfactory cash-flow in all possible cases.

/s/ Hirashi Oyama

"I have read your memorandum," said Kijin in his hoarse voice, "and I have some questions. Suppose Rosinante's utility is not sufficient to repay the Ecufiscale loan, what then?"

"We default, of course," said Oyama. "I myself will recommend it."

"Ah. I see. And you very properly did not put such a suggestion in writing." Kijin nodded. "You hope to sacrifice Rosinante to save the other two?"

"Of course, sir. Rosinante is lost in any event." Oyama smiled politely, as if such a truth were so obvious as to be unworthy of utterance.

"The next question is, where will you get twenty-five hundred women?"

"Hong Kong, possibly, or Shanghai. This is the third year the Chinese have had a poor wheat crop, and our project would be oversubscribed with volunteers. We could even require a knowledge of English as a condition for going."

"Perhaps." Kijin appeared doubtful. "Why not try to do something for your own country?"

"Recruit Japanese girls to marry Texicans?" Oyama was scandalized.

"No, no! We have an overlarge population of Korean nationals in Japan. Why not recruit from them?" Kijin asked. "That way there is no need to go across national borders."

"Very true, sir," said Oyama enthusiastically, "and security and transportation will be much easier. And in this case, Mitsui's interests coincide with theirs." He smiled. "Korean girls may find that hard to believe."

"No matter. They will come anyway." He coughed into his hand. "So. It would appear that Admiral Kogo is willing to gamble a shuttle load if you are prepared to write off Mundito Rosinante." Kijin produced a handkerchief and coughed again. "The first estimated flight time is in ten days, May twelfth. *If* you can find twenty-five hundred young women, and *if* you can get them on board the shuttle, and *if* the ozone layer behaves properly, then you have until May fourteenth to attempt this rash scheme." He looked at the clock on his office wall. "It's late. Would you like to join me for a few drinks?"

# CHAPTER 8

"This is the setup," said the technician. "We spotted a dozen telecon sets around the billets in the cassette magazine, and we told the Texicans you'd be answering questions one on one after the show. You finish with one group, you push the button for the next. Ten through twenty-one on the control, here."

"What about the other numbers?" asked Cantrell.

"They aren't hooked up. Do you want me to tape them over?" Cantrell shook his head.

"No. I'll remember. I'll just go down in sequence, is all."

"No sweat," said the technician. "Come back in about thirty-five minutes. The second movie still has about forty minutes left to run."

Cantrell walked down the hall to the Stateside Café and ordered a draft Guinness.

"I'm sorry, sir," said the robot waiter, "we haven't been able to get enough barley for our microbrewery, and we ran out of beer."

"I see," said Cantrell.

"It's all those extra mouths to feed," said the waiter. "But I have been assured that the shortage is temporary."

"I'm sure it will be," agreed Cantrell, "just the matter of a day or two. How about coffee and rye toast?"

"Of course, sir. Will you have your coffee black, as usual?"

Cantrell was back in the broadcast room ten minutes before he was due to speak, watching the audience watching the end of an old, familiar movie and nursing a foam plastic cup of coffee. Then he was on, and he pressed button ten. His telecon screen showed a group of about two hundred young men watching him with close attention.

"Good evening. My name is Charles C. Cantrell, and I am the project manager here at Mundito Rosinante. The first film you saw was a news update from Texas, your home until very recently, covering what happened since you left so unexpectedly. It was news to me, too. I was born and raised in Santa Fe, New Mexico, but it's been a long time, and I haven't kept in touch. I can't answer any questions like 'Who blew up the governor?' " There was a general laugh. "The second film you saw was a presentation for bankers and other moneyed illiterates. It shows what and where Mundito Rosinante is, and how it got started, and why we expect to make lots and lots of money with it. This I have lived with. This is where you now are. And I will try to answer your questions about this. First question, please. The gentleman in the black T-shirt."

"Mr. Cantrell, sir, what are we going to be doing here?"

"That's a good question. In the short haul, you'll be raising your own food. Eventually . . . well, we're putting *Hevea brasiliensis* in purlin three, a rubber plantation, and so some of you may wind up working in rubber. However, once the construction work is finished, *I* will be moving on, so I don't really have a hand on your future." He pressed button eleven and looked at a new group.

"The gentleman with the soupstrainer mustache, please."

"Ah, sir, the movie said this place was only begun, but it looks finished to me. Isn't it done yet?"

"Well, it's an old movie, but when you say 'done,' there is done and then there is *done*. When I was a kid, I built a plastic ship model. It was the *Cutty Sark*, a clipper ship, and it took me a week to paint it, and put the hull together, and the masts in, and the spars on, and all the little fiddling pieces you glue on. It was done. But it wasn't *done* until I put on the rigging. Black thread for the standing rigging. Brown thread for the running rigging. The rigging took two weeks. Are we done with Mundito Rosinante? Sort of. We're working on the stuff that can't be tackled until you have stabilized gravity and air pressure at equilibrium. The plumbing, and wiring, and ductwork. The irrigation systems, riparian loops, and sewage treatment plants. A million fiddling details. The rigging, if you will. You, sir—yes, you in the plaid shirt."

"The ship didn't give us any mail, or let us write home. Will we get our mail?"

"Yes. We have thousands of letters in microfiche format

brought over from the ship, but we don't have the paper to print them up on. I'll see that you get readers and that your mail gets distributed." He hit button number twelve.

"The food is awful! What are you going to do about it? Sir?"

"We'll work you up the food chain as fast as we can," replied Cantrell, "but the first results you'll see will be in about sixty days with the shrimp." A cheer went up. "It will take about ninety days for the boost in egg production to show."

Someone called out, "Shell eggs?"

"That's the way the hens lay them," said Cantrell. "The wheat and soybeans will come in about one hundred twenty days, and the meat animals in two to three years." He pushed button thirteen. This group was smaller, and about half women, the only women he had seen so far.

"The lady in the denim jacket," he said.

"What is this 'cassette magazine' we're in?"

"It's where we stored the cassettes," said Cantrell. "The rolls of sheet steel or sheet aluminum on the Shelob spools."

"Shelob spools?"

"The Shelobs are the big beam spinners," he explained. "They spun sheet metal on the spools—the cassettes—into beams for construction. The blonde with the red bandanna."

"In school we learned that glass windows could be nine or ten millimeters thick, but your windows are thirty millimeters thick. Why is that?"

"I see you read the blueprints in the movie," said Cantrell. "It has to do with the way we put the windows together, the glass temperature and the time we took. We could have made the windows nine millimeters thick, but it would have taken maybe ten times as long, and since we made the glass locally, it was cheaper to make it thirty millimeters."

"I have another question," she said. "How does the air circulate in those long purlins? I mean, I learned in school . . ."

"We pump hot, moist air through the berm tanks to the radiators on the outer caps," Cantrell said. "The water condenses out for the purlin water supply, the heat radiates off into space, and we have a steady flow of cool, dry air flowing down from the outer cap. Okay?"

"Okay," she agreed, smiling, "but why are they called 'berm tanks'?"

"A berm is a shoulder of earth against a wall," Cantrell said. "The berm tank runs like a shoulder of earth against the purlin window, so it keeps you from looking over the edge, and it protects the long axis seam between purlin window and purlin plate. You, sir, with the mustache."

"A purlin is another name for a roof beam. How did the name come to be applied to these structures inside?"

Cantrell sighed. "Mordecai Rubenstein once told me that in the early models they built the structural supports in the center and worked outward. Those supports were called purlins, so I suppose that in time all the major inner structure came to be called purlin this and purlin that. But I don't know. Yes, ma'am."

"There is a project called Sancho Panza, but no asteroid of that name. Why is that?"

"I expect we ran out of asteroids before we ran out of projects, ma'am," replied Cantrell with the utmost courtesy. "Sir?"

"Why are the purlins separate inside the envelope of the mundito?"

"The bankers asked the same question. The structure is much stronger, for one thing, and more resistant to damage or sabotage."

"*Try* to kick a wooden shoe through a window three centimeters thick!" someone said, to general laughter.

"Or seven thousand meters above your head," said Cantrell. "Actually, it was a change order from Mitsui, early on in the project. That's just the way they wanted it." He pushed button fourteen with some reluctance.

"Is there anything to drink out here besides water."

"We're setting up a microbrewery. You will get a beer ration of about half a liter per person per week until after the grain harvest is in, when the supply should be ample." A small ripple of applause. "You, sir, with the leather vest."

"When are they going to get some women up here?"

"I don't know. Rosinante is a joint project: Mitsui and Scadiwa. You all are from Scadiwa. When Mitsui sends up their people, maybe they'll send along some extra women. Maybe." He pushed button fifteen. "The gentleman in khaki shorts, please."

"When are we going to move into our permanent quarters?"

"About two weeks. We'll try to set it up for you as fast as we can. I'll take one more question. You, sir."

"Couldn't we go home in the ship that brought us here?"

"*The Star of Mexicali* isn't bound for Tellus. It's hauling our Shelobs—the big beam spinners—on to Phobos, and the mirror-making machines are en route to one of Mitsui's projects orbiting Ceres."

"I mean, when are we going home?" the boy asked.

"I don't know. In a year or two, most likely." They were never going home, probably, but it wouldn't do to say it out loud.

# CHAPTER 9

Laputa is in stationary orbit over Midway Island, drawing the shuttle traffic from the Pacific coast of Asia, and from the western NAU, to transfer to the carriers of high space. Originally it had been an orbital fortress, but today the military presence was largely administrative.

Dr. Marian Yashon sat among the gracefully sculpted boxwoods of Hotel Laputa's formal garden with Corporate Skaskash. Skaskash was a quite remarkable collection of hardware, firmware, software, and gossamer opinion whose functions had been honed and refined in the wars, reorganizations, and internecine power struggles at the Tellurbank. As a corporation and a legal person, Skaskash held a Universal CPA's license, and was entitled to practice forensic statistics. It was also fluent in Chinese, Japanese, English, French, and Spanish to the extent that it could simultaneously translate from any one to any other one. Not by accident, Corporate Skaskash owned 43 percent of Skaskash, Inc., while Ecufiscale Tellurbank owned 47 percent. It was very conscious of the 10 percent that Odarchenko had given Marian as a nongoing-away present, and was extending her quite extraordinary courtesy in consequence. They had been playing Go for three days while they waited for the rest of the team to arrive, and Skaskash had discovered that its best efforts were insufficient to win. Eventually they settled on a five-stone handicap, and sat in the garden playing Go to kill time. Skaskash, of course, was also checking arrival times, and passenger lists, and periodically checking with the home office to find what progress the other team members were making. It also read the papers and magazines Dr. Yashon read, and related material that she didn't read and conversed.

"Shall we go down and meet the Quemoy Shuttle?" suggested Skaskash, cutting a line Marian had been extending toward a knot of white stones.

"Are any of our people on it?" she asked, playing a stone to form a Tiger's Mouth at the end of the cut line.

"No," said Skaskash, studying the board. "However, it will be the last shuttle for ten days or so, until the ozone recoups its losses." It placed an outpost on the other side of the board.

"Is the *Sacred Plum Blossom* still waiting for cargo before departure?" Dr. Yashon asked.

Skaskash checked. "The *Secular Plum Blossom*. No, it isn't. ETD is 0225 tomorrow. We seem to be the whole team, in this case." It paused a moment. "Should I call Colonel Mohammed to verify our orders?"

"No—no. If we are wanted somewhere else, it is their obligation to send us instructions. You might send down the estimated time of departure, though. Keep the home office informed and all that."

"CYA," agreed Skaskash. "It's done. Would you like hard copy?"

"What for? You've filed it, haven't you?"

They were starting the next game when an oriental girl about sixteen years old came over and asked very politely, in English, if she could watch.

"It would be my pleasure," said Skaskash in Japanese. "Won't you sit down, please." The girl giggled and sat down at the table. As she did so, another girl in the same uniform—white slacks, white shirt, white tennis shoes, navy-blue windbreaker with white piping, and a crimson ascot—came up.

"What are you doing, Mishi?" she asked in halting English.

"I invited Mishi to watch our Go game," Skaskash told her in Japanese. "If you also wish to watch, you are welcome to do so." The second girl giggled.

"Why are you speaking English?" asked Dr. Yashon.

"Because we must practice so our English is very good, Honorable Lady," said Mishi carefully. "We are going to a far-off place to marry American men for husband, and so we must learn to English speak."

"We came here on the Quemoy Shuttle," added the other girl, "and in a few hours we leave on the *Secular Plum Blossom*." She giggled nervously. "It is very exciting," she added. Dr. Yashon's belt phone sounded, and she answered it.

"The Quemoy Shuttle was a Mitsui charter," Skaskash told her over the phone, "carrying twenty-five hundred young ladies from Japan. Small bet that they are Rosinante bound."

"No bet," Dr. Yashon told the phone, and closed it. "We also are taking the *Secular Plum Blossom*," she told the girls, "and will be traveling with you as far as Mundito Rosinante." She smiled and offered her hand to Mishi, who took it, a little startled. "My name is Marian Yashon," she said, "and this is Corporate Skaskash." The two girls giggled and gave their names and giggled again. By the time the final game of Go ended, the garden was full of navy-blue windbreakers with white piping.

# CHAPTER 10

The Green Ballroom of La Grande Schyler Hotel was filled well beyond the capacity of the air-conditioning to cool. On stage, Sergio Gonzales and his Grosso Mariachis played one-step arrangements of Strauss waltzes, a dance craze Gonzales had done much to make popular. Overhead, the chandelier, a cunning arrangement of cut crystal, prisms, and mirrors, turned on well-lubricated bearings and changed shape, ever so slowly, writhing and seething, alive with prismatic lights and stabbing flashes of pure color. Barely short of hypnotic, it listened to the music and danced with it. For a real Strauss waltz, the hotel management would have turned it off.

Hirashi Oyama of Mitsui handed Isoruku Llamamoto of the Tellurbank a glass of California champagne, one of the world's premium vintages, and raised his own glass in a toast.

"I've been curious about your name since I first saw it," Oyama said. "I hope no offense is given if I ask how the *Y* came to be *Ll*."

"None at all," replied Llamamoto. "My father went to Cambridge, where he came under the influence of a contemporary Welsh poet, and in a witty—and perhaps romantic—gesture he changed his name so. Father wrote bad poetry and fair reviews for a season, until my grandfather took him home to an arranged marriage with my mother. He began to drink heavily, and died shortly after I was born. I was raised in the house of his parents, and when I came of age, I took his spelling of my name to honor his memory." He sipped his champagne, and smiled a barely minimum smile. "The fact that it enraged my honorable grandfather could not, of course, have influenced my decision."

"Ah, Oyama! Llamamoto!" Kijin made his way through the crowd with a strikingly beautiful woman. "Allow me to present Marina Elena Retsinoupolis, better known as Marina Retsina." Oyama took her hand and stammered something inane, Llamamoto, a trifle more poised, managed to smile as he shook her hand. Then Kijin and the actress moved off through the crowd.

"What a body," whispered Oyama, "and what a beautiful face."

"It isn't generally known," said Llamamoto, "but Hsu Ko Jing, our president, is a fan of hers. He has all her movies in his library."

"Hsu Ko Jing is a pig!" Marina hissed at Kijin.

"You set him up beautifully," he replied. "Now just stay out of sight. And listen to the monitor to avoid any foul-up when you come on at midnight to do your act."

Trembling with excitement, the president of Ecufiscale Tellurbank let himself into Marina Retsina's private room with the key she had given him.

"Old Jing's right on schedule," said a technician, watching a TV monitor. "Now give him a few minutes and enter with the other key, right?"

"Of course right," said a woman who looked very much like Marina Retsina, in a voice that sounded exactly like Marina Retsina's.

"You've got the lip synch down pat," said the technician approvingly. "Just let the computer do the talking and you've got it made."

"Do you really think he's going to act out one of my old movie scenes?" asked the computer in Retsina's voice.

The technician nodded. "Oh, hell, yes. You don't suppose he's going to ad lib his own dialogue, do you? Probably the sexual assault in *Orange Blossom Honey*—the room matches the set somewhat, and it's one of his favorites." She checked the makeup blending the computer's speakers with the woman's skin one last time. "If he says 'You've been gone for hours!' when you walk in, you'll be home free. You'll be on the bed with your dress over your head in no time."

The woman nodded. "No problem with lip synch on ad libs," she said in her own voice.

"Lots of verbal protest," said Retsina's voice, "while the

body struggles weakly and ineffectively, and then submits. Okay, body, let's do our thing."

The woman who looked like Marina Retsina stood up and checked herself in the mirror, winked at the technician, and went out to earn her pay.

Kijin and Admiral Kogo sat at a stage side table waiting for Marina Retsina to come on, Kogo smoking a cigar, Kijin drinking scotch and soda. Hsu Ko Jing made his way through the crowd and joined them, blotting his forehead with a handkerchief.

"How did it go?" asked Kogo. Hsu smiled, making dimples in his fat.

"Very well, She played a scene from *Orange Blossom Honey* with me. You know, she can make the most banal dialogue sound alive and fresh." He took out pipe and pouch, and carefully began to tamp the rough-cut burley into the bowl of his briar.

Kijin laughed. "Listen," he said, "when I finish this drink, I'll be shit-faced drunk, but while I remember, would you initial this waiver we discussed earlier?" He fumbled in his coat pocket and took out a sheet of paper folded lengthwise. The Tellurbank's president unfolded it and put on his glasses. It read: "Inspection prior to loan approval is hereby waived for Icarus-Mitsui, L-5 Mitsui IV, and Rosinante–Mitsui Scadiwa, once staffing is complete in each case." Hsu lit his pipe, and got it going to his satisfaction. Then he carefully put pouch and matches back in his pocket. Finally, he felt around for a pen. Kijin felt like screaming "Here is my pen!" but he clenched his hands under the table, and felt very proud that he gave no sign of the anxiety he felt. Kogo blandly watched a smoke ring he had blown. Finally, Hsu Ko Jing produced a pen, removed the cap, and signed the waiver with a flourish. Kogo signed it as a witness, and dated it. As if on cue, the bouzouki band struck up "Iskedara," and Marina Retsina made her entrance to thunderous applause. She held up her hand and the audience fell silent.

"It is my very great pleasure tonight to announce that I have signed to play the role of Melina Mercouri in *I Was Born Greek*. Production will begin in six weeks." More applause, and the band went into "Never on Sunday."

Kijin put the waiver in his pocket, finished his drink, and leaned back to watch the chandelier go crazy.

# CHAPTER 11

Code 2107643100.14
Secular Plum Blossom, Rm 4110
July 4, 2039

Dear Ras,

When I was a little girl, it was on this date that I arrived at Dulles Airport in what was then the United States with my parents. It had been a long dull trip, and it. was a long dull wait to go through Customs, and when we got to the hotel I was cranky and not sleepy, so we all took the subway to the Washington Monument to see the fireworks. We arrived shortly before the first salute went up, and over in Virginia (my mother told me) there were big black clouds and flashes of lightning. The rain was coming, so they shot off 45 minutes' worth of fireworks in ten, the most wonderful thing I had ever seen! And after that incredible barrage ended, the sound rolled over me for another few seconds. And when it stopped, there was absolute silence for a moment, and then a lightning bolt hit the Monument, louder than all that had gone before, and the rain came down in torrents.

NAU no longer honors the Fourth of July, although the people continue to celebrate it unofficially, and I feel the loss. To be sure, I carry an Israeli passport as I travel on the Tellurbank's business, but Israel is now pickled in the sour brine of theology, and I could never live there, so why do I miss the fireworks of my youth?

Skaskash has taken over the ship's closed-circuit TV, and has been giving English lessons and tutoring in shifts around the clock. The missionary woman nominally in charge is a saintly incompetent, *so* pleased that her little girls are being kept out of trouble. Meanwhile, Skaskash is compiling biographical data, and when we are in communication range of Rosinante (ship to station, not via some expensive relay) will set up as matchmaker. The girls seem very pleased with this, and as a result they all know me, and as the Director of Corporate Skaskash, I command the utmost respect. To poor Mrs. Smith-Bakersfield they are barely polite.

For what it's worth, Skaskash says that all the girls are of Korean descent. Intuitively, although I turned in my intuition for logical analysis a long time ago, this suggests that Mitsui holds the project in minimum high esteem. I don't like it.

July 5, 2039

I had a strange dream just before waking. I was playing poker in a Western saloon, like the one in Disneyworld, when a chimera, with the head of a lion and the body of a bear, sat down at the table. All the other players threw in a red chip to begin play, and the chimera threw in a red rose. Then I dealt the cards, and the betting was very heavy, and when it was time to show the cards, the chimera grabbed the pot and ran off, leaving the rose on the table.

I awoke feeling terribly disturbed. Skaskash suggests that rose-in-ante is an obvious meaning, and that the chimera is Mitsui-Scadiwa. If so, my subconscious, at least, is worried that they are going to abandon the rose-in-ante and run off with our loan, the pot.

You see what happens when you order me not to begin work before we actually arrive on the site? Well, ETA is August 15, so we will sit tight and see what we find. Meanwhile, I am reviewing the plans with Skaskash so that I can tell what I am looking at . . . eventually.

Shalom,
/s/ Marian

From the log of the *Secular Plum Blossom.*

8/15/39 2459:   Achieved zero velocity relative to MR as ordered. Docking maneuvers begin. Distance 1542 meters, angle between MR and SPB axes of rotation 28°40'.

| 8/16/39 0312: | Spin jets frozen at right angles to anti-spin direction, where they had been used as auxiliary braking jets after main jets focusing magnet lost supercooling. |
| --- | --- |
| 0315: | Begin internal ballistic flywheels to damp rotation. |
| 1209: | Rotation stopped. Distance 1504 meters. |
| 1330: | Y-axis and Z-axis flywheels have aligned axes of rotation. X-axis flywheel will not start to match SPB's rotation to MR's. |
| 1342: | X-axis flywheel delaminated. Begin replacement of X-axis flywheel with Z-axis flywheel, since spare is wrong size. |
| 1548: | Flywheel replaced. Begin matching MR's rotation. Distance 1468 meters to MR. |
| 1807: | Rotation matches. Explosive delamination of X-axis flywheel on braking. No casualties. |
| 1810: | MR's docking crew extends braking beams. Distance 1420 meters. |
| 1814: | Braking cables secured to outfacing eye-bolts. Tug line extended. |
| 1825: | MR reports tug line secure |
| 2350: | Contact with loading dock/#2 cargo hold. |
| 2425: | Annular seal tumesced at contact point. MR docking crew reports seal is tight. |
| 2455: | Pressure equalized, #2 cargo hold airlock opens. |
| 8/17/39 0015: | Begin discharging supercargo. Chief Engineer MacInterff submits formal resignation. |
| 0018: | Capt. Furukawa to sickbay with broken nose. |

As soon as the airlock opened, the supercargo, 2,500 nubile oriental females, came swarming out like a flock of birds, some in underwear, some in the buff, all carrying their travel bags with their dress whites carefully preserved for the end of the journey. The elevator to the number-one purlin bay was plainly visible, and clearly marked. A sign in glowing neon lights said: "Welcome to Rosinante" in red, and underneath in blue, "We rejoy in you arrival" in Japanese characters. A green horse on a white field ran awkwardly in place, looking like a candidate for the glue factory. Red, white, and blue bunting decorated the sides of the elevator, and above it, on the massive reel housing, were displayed the banners of Japan, Korea, the North American Union, Texas, and the Stars and Bars of the Confederacy. The Stars and Stripes of the old regime still roused high emotions and was never displayed officially.

On the elevator, a freight elevator capable of moving a fully assembled Shelob beam spinner, was a rack of seats, twenty by twenty-five stacked five high, looking lost and rather small in the elevator's vastness. The elevator was not exactly in zero gravity, but it wasn't far from it, and the girls had no trouble getting into their places. In the back of the elevator a row of portable toilets had been set up, and a wall of mirrors. There would be time enough; the elevator took two hours ten minutes to reach the end of its journey.

"Have we got everybody?" asked Mrs. Smith-Bakersfield.

"Mishi Sung is bringing up the last stragglers now," said Skaskash. "This is truly the last leg of the journey, you know. *They* are coming to what they must make home, and when they get off the elevator they will be there."

"I would have thought there would be a welcoming committee," the Missionary Lady said a bit petulantly.

"There will be," said Dr. Yashon, "when we get off the elevator. Ask Skaskash, here."

"Quite true, ma'am," replied the computer. "The whole community is falling out to celebrate our arrival, despite the lateness of the hour."

"Why, it will be two thirty or three in the morning when we arrive," said Mrs. Smith-Bakersfield, looking at her watch, "and black as pitch, I shouldn't wonder. Do they want a parade by street lights?"

"I think they will turn on the sun for us," said Skaskash, "as a mark of how they hope we will lighten their lives."

"The heathen do not know The Light when it shines in their willfully darkened eyes," she said, looking reproachfully at Marian Yashon.

"How are you doing at converting Skaskash?" asked Dr. Yashon. Then Mishi Sung came up with the last members of their party, and the elevator doors began to slowly close.

"What did you mean: 'Turn on the sun'?" asked Mrs. Smith-Bakersfield.

"Exactly that," Skaskash replied. "They do it with mirrors, of course."

When the elevator doors opened, bright sunlight poured in, and a band—snare drums, field drums, flutes, fifes, and bagpipes—was playing. As the girls began to get out of the rack of seats, the band was playing "Amazing Grace," and when they had formed up into a semiorderly mass and started walking across the field to the blue-striped pavilion where refreshments were waiting, the band struck up "Dixie." Skaskash had taught the girls the song in the course of shipboard English lessons, and they began to sing it.

Across the field, behind a rope barrier, waited their men. Somebody gave a rebel yell, a wild ululating cry, and others took it up. Then the rope barrier went down, and the men were running across the field, some singing, some yelling, and some just running. Then there was a confused melee, as Texicans and Japanese-Koreans sorted themselves out into the pairs Skaskash had worked so diligently to sort out. Marian looked at the Missionary Lady in surprise.

"Why, Willie," she exclaimed, "you're crying!"

"I always cry at weddings," she said, blowing her nose.

# CHAPTER 12

A default is a nonevent, promised money that is not paid, a due date unmet, silence where the jingle of coins was expected. The consequences of default involve the use of force, actual or implicit. A sofa repossessed, a tenant evicted, a welcher beaten.

Curiously, money spent to buy dinner is different from money spent to buy a house. Snow thrown as a snowball is different from snow shoveled laboriously out of the driveway. Money, en masse, acquires singular properties, as snow, blowing through the air in cold, crystalline flakes, may in time be transmuted to spring floods, or, if the climate is right, to the ponderous and inexorable glacier.

Defaulting a glacier is different from defaulting a snowball.

Colonel Ras Mohammed sat in his office, rumple-suited and baggy eyed, looking over a pad of legal-sized foolscap he had been working on. Finally he put on a pair of dark glasses and cued the television recorder.

"Shalom, Marian," he began. "This is by way of being an apology and an explanation, although you always understood me well enough so that perhaps I will be explaining something other than I imagine.

"First, I apologize for putting you in your present position, the awkward and useless position you now hold. President Hsu never insisted on you, he only suggested that you would be a good choice, and to my immediate loss and eternal shame, I agreed. I should have kept you, and I could have.

"Second, on August sixteenth, Mitsui came in with three waivers of inspection, including one for Mitsui-Scadiwa's Mundito Rosinante, and when we confirmed that two were already staffed, and that the *Secular Plum Blossom* had reached zero velocity with respect to Rosinante—Mundito Rosinante—on the fifteenth, I approved the loan. I had no choice, but forgive me for not telling you. I was embarrassed, and to spare myself pain, I said nothing. Beyond measure, I could have used the counsel that I kept you from giving.

"Yesterday, October second, at close of business, Mitsui-Scadiwa informed us that 'due to the unique staffing at Rosinante' they were defaulting the loan, and that title was reverting to the Tellurbank automatically.

"When we pulled the file, the waiver was gone, and the copies of the waiver were also gone, and it will not be found, for President Hsu swears that he never signed such a document.

"The defaulted loan was approved on my sole responsibility, and worse, I acted against the advice of my subordinates to do so. Can you imagine what advice I am guilty of acting against? Your dream, the chimera, with the rose-in-ante, is the evidence that I should have taken into account to overrule President Hsu!

"The waiver was an accomplished fact, but with your guidance it could have been accomplished differently.

"Tomorrow, this office will be occupied by S. A. Odarchenko of Ukrainia, a detestable man, an antisemite in a sly way, but a clever and an effective operator." Colonel Mohammed removed his glasses and rubbed his eyes.

"I have no further orders for you, and no suggestions. Marian, I am sorry, I am so sorry." He looked directly at the camera, and repeated: "I am *so* sorry."

The news of default was like a pebble tossed into a still pond, the ripples began to spread in all directions. And the financial writers sought an explanation.

The *Times* of London paired it with a story from the Orbital Solar Observatory. The hard kernel of fact in the story was that the sunspots so recently returned after a three-year leave of absence were moving 3.5 percent faster than they had before, and that the sun's rotation was therefore that much faster. The speculation that tied it to the financial page was the invocation of archaic observations to support speculation that the sun was on the verge of a new Maunder Minimum. The Maunder Minimum, as the financial writer was at pains to explain, was a seventy-year period when there were no sunspots, and that Mitsui-

Scadiwa knew this, and defaulted to get out of the space manufacturing business because in the absence of sunspots, the ozone layer would not support sufficient space traffic to make commerce profitable.

The *New York Times* financial writer assigned the Rosinante default story asked the science writer he was living with for a possible explanation, and she dug into her pile of review copies and came up with *Ozone and Climate: An Investigation of the Effects of Human Intervention on the Ozone Layer on World Climate*, a stupefying dull publication of statistics and graphs. She leafed through the book until she found the chapter titled: "Is the World-wide Drought a Side Effect of Space Travel?"

"What does that mean?" asked the financial writer.

"It means that what's his face thinks that the droughts of the last decade or so are the direct result of keeping the ozone layer down by flying space shuttles through it," said the science writer.

"Hey, I can use that!" said the financial writer. "Can you do me a review to go with my story?"

"Sure I can. I've read the book already," she said. "Ask your editor if he wants it, and if he does, I'll have it for you by deadline."

Other papers favored other theories, but those were the most popular. In time, it was noticed that they were not contradictory.

On the seventh day, October 9, Krupp-Europa Farmacia Cie. defaulted on their DNA recombinant facility. The operation had been marginal from the very beginning, and recent tax legislation had simply made the L-5 location uneconomical, said Krupp-Europa. The explanation happened to be completely true. It was, all the same, heavily discounted on the world's financial pages.

On October 10, the next day, it was officially announced that the North American wheat harvest was 3 percent below the year before, 12 percent below projections at the start of the year.

Wheat prices rose sharply on the news, and wheat futures for March and July went through the ceiling.

The secretary of NAUGA-Agriculture dealt vigorously with the impending crisis. She went on nationwide TV waving a copy of *Ozone and Climate* and called for a two-year moratorium on shuttle flights. She blamed the poor wheat crop on the weather, and the weather on the space shuttles. Her statistic that the loss in NAU wheat production exceeded the value of all imports from space during crop year 38–39 was universally quoted. It was specious, but it was quoted, and remembered, and in time became part of folklore.

The secretary recognized, of course, that she would neither produce wheat nor lower prices in this fashion. However, by taking swift, visible action she gave the appearance of managing a crisis that fell in her area of responsibility. It did not matter that she was proposing a simple-minded solution to a complex, difficult, and intractable problem. Her proposal was easily understood, and clear to everybody. By thus appearing to manage, she avoided the real crisis, which would have been the Congressional investigation of those NAUGA-Agriculture policies that led to the shortfall in wheat production. The policies had not been bad, but in hindsight they should have been different. Thus did the secretary defend her agency and her tenure.

It is a maxim of the Zen Bureaucrat that you cannot do only one thing. In the defense of her agency, the secretary lent official credence to a highly speculative theory. In time this would be corrected; NAUGA-Air Space would shortly produce a complete and elegant demolition job.

In mid October, however, it led investors to recognize that space had been overbuilt, oversold, and—the unkindest cut of all—overvalued. Grossly overvalued.

This perception led to the wholesale cancellation of space building projects, at least civilian space building projects, and several marginally profitable munditos followed Mundito Rosinante into default.

Ecufiscale Tellurbank reeled. The loss of cash flow from the defaulted loans was endurable, but simultaneously the eicu came under heavy speculative pressure from the international banks, Ecufiscale's blood brothers and long-time collaborators. What the international bankers saw was first, that the eicu was a piece of paper backed with title to a lot of worthless real estate, second, that no single government would support the Tellurbank when push came to shove, and third, that they themselves were holding an awful lot of the stuff.

The Tellurbank drew on its reserves of national currencies, suddenly "hard" currencies, and on its lines of credit until they were spent. Useless, the currency it had issued so freely came pouring in for redemption. In desperation the Tellurbank sought to negotiate the sale of some of the defaulted properties at inflated prices to restore confidence in the eicu. NAUGA-War turned them down, as did NAUGA-Air and Space. Negotiations with NAUGA-Treasury collapsed when they were leaked to the press, and on October 29, 2039, Ecufiscale Tellurbank closed its doors.

The world economy, slumping, slumped a little deeper. The North American Union, having a dominant position in space construction, suffered the pangs of statistical setbacks and the pains of paper losses more than most. Even in the NAU, however, the effects were heavily buffered. The biggest losers were the heaviest investors, government agencies and large corporations. The consumers felt the rise in wheat prices more.

# CHAPTER 13

Cantrell was drinking black coffee in the Stateside Café and studying inspection reports, when Marian Yashon walked over to his table.

"Good morning, Charles," she said. "May I join you?"

"Sure, Tiger. Have a seat." He stacked the reports to one side and looked at her rather thoughtfully. "This isn't really your time of day, is it?"

The robot waiter took her order for rye toast and a pot of tea and moved silently off.

"I guess not," Marian said, "although maybe it is. I'm a night person, and I haven't slept, so here I am at breakfast. In the old days I'd have steak and eggs and home fries, and tea with a spoonful of cherry preserves. Maybe a piece of apple pie with cheddar cheese later. Now I have to watch my weight."

"Why," asked Cantrell, picking up his cue, "didn't you sleep?"

"I got a videotaped transmission from my boss. My ex-boss, actually. I won't go into detail, but he said, and I confirmed, that the new head of my department is S. A. Odarchenko."

"You say the name like I should know it," Cantrell said. "What about him, or her, as the case may be?"

"Him. Stepan Alexandrovitch. If I thought there was any chance that he wouldn't fire me, I'd quit."

"Sweetly reasonable, as always, Tiger. What can I do for you?"

"Can you use a strategist? I'll tell you straight: Colonel Mohammed loved me because I kept him out of trouble, and he hated me because I stopped him from doing the dumb, or thoughtless, or reckless things he wanted to do."

"What I want to do is build. The bigger the better."

Cantrell sipped his coffee and studied her. "You want a job, Tiger?" The robot waiter came over and refilled his cup. "I imagine I could use you, perhaps in union negotiations. I could use Corporate Skaskash, too, if I could get him. But what about the propriety of hiring the team that's doing the Tellurbank's loan authorization study? It doesn't matter whether I take you on before or after the event, it wouldn't look—you should pardon the expression—kosher."

The robot waiter served Marian her tea and toast.

"The loan authorization study? The one I'm still working on? Hah! That loan was approved before I ever got off the ship. Colonel Mohammed didn't get around to telling me until just before the end, is all!"

Cantrell raised his cup. "A toast to makework," he offered.

"Confusion to idiots in high places," she replied.

"My inclination is to hire," he said at last, "particularly if you bring along Corporate Skaskash. I'd have to puzzle out how to fit you in, because to put the best possible face on the matter, Tiger, your skills and talents are a little . . . ah, incongruous to our business."

"There's no hurry," she said, "just think it over. And Skaskash *will* sign if I do."

Cantrell sat and watched her eat her toast. "I'll think about it," he said finally, "and while you wait for Odarchenko to sign your pink slip, why don't you check out our shop to see what you might wind up doing."

She refilled her teacup. "It wouldn't be the first time I wrote my own job description, Charles. There is one other thing you should know. After Mitsui-Scadiwa got their loan, they defaulted." She smiled. "I expect you'll get the word in a day or two."

"Oh, really?" Charles C. Cantrell seemed genuinely puzzled. "The project is in pretty damn good shape, as you well know. Once the supercritical $CO_2$ purging valves are reversed on the charcoal filters, the left side is done."

"I know that purlins one, two, and three are the left side of the mundito, but why is it called that?"

"Because of the rotation. The mundito has two cylinders rotating in opposite directions for stability. Right and left handed. You point your thumbs at the sun, and your fingers point in the direction of the spin. The left side cylinder is done, except for those valves installed backward. Why would they default?"

"For strategic reasons," said Marian, pouring more tea.

"A resident strategist might be useful at that," Cantrell conceded. "Particularly if she had a working knowledge of our new owners."

"Compliments of the management, ma'am," the telephone man told Mrs. Smith-Bakersfield. "We have an order to put this teleconference display screen upside your old phone."

"What is it?" asked the hopelessly nontechnical missionary lady.

"The screen, here, 132 by 170 centimeters, sits against the wall. It's a little curved, see, and the projector sits in front of it like one pedestal on this little coffee table. The camera is in the other pedestal, and the lenses are these little roundels along the table's edge facing you. Lookit, right here. The whole thang connects with your phone on a fiber-optic cable, and you have to turn this switch to C for conference—"

"How do I know to turn the switch on?"

"Your phone rings, lady. The other party asks for a conference call, that's all you need."

"What are the other positions?"

"Right, lady. Off is O, on the right, the TV is for cable television, in the middle. Put it on TV and touch the channel number you want on your phone, and you got it. On the left is C, for conference."

"What is"—she smiled vaguely—"I'm not very clever about machines, you know. What is a conference call?"

"Why, lady, the screen lights up to show you the other party or parties, maybe. And you talk to them just like they were there. Lookit, I'll show you." He ran a series of tests, made an adjustment, and called his supervisor.

"Looks good," said the super. "Did you check the grounding? Some of the ground lines are dead over there."

"Yeah, no problem."

"Okay, you have two more phones in that building, then see about fixing the big TV set in the Tommy Riley Bar and Grill." She checked her list for something and turned her set off.

"There you are, ma'am," said the installer, leaving with

his box of tools. He tipped his hat at the door. "She's working fine."

Mrs. Smith-Bakersfield looked in bewilderment at the object intruding in her living room for a moment. Then her phone rang, and she picked it up.

"Hello, Willie, this is Corporate Skaskash," said a voice that sounded like Humphrey Bogart. "May we have a conference call, please?"

# CHAPTER 14

A few days later a letter arrived. Technically, it was a tele-communication printed as hard copy, but it was from the central office, and for such missives the printer generated its copy on letterhead. This particular letterhead had been designed as part of an ad campaign. Roman Classic type in deep scarlet, G.Y. FOX CONSTRUCTION COMPANY, INC. framed a blue line drawing of an early model mundito on fluorescent white bond paper. Mason Fox had liked the campaign because he had modeled the executive holding the so-visible letterhead. Being the nephew of George Ypsilanti Fox, he had in time become the chief executive officer of Gyfox.

October 7, 2039

Dear Charles:

We all have been extremely pleased with your work on Project Rosinante. The economic situation, unfortunately, is not too good for space construction right now.

You're fired.

The union too, Mitbestimmung and all.

Unless, of course, we can maybe cut a deal. The alternative to riffing your collective ass is to spin off Rosinante Division as a separate company.

Attachment I is a list of Rosinante, Inc.'s, assets and obligations. We will give you 51 percent of that pitiful lemon in return for the Gyfox stock you acquired when we bought up C.C. Cantrell Enterprises.

But! you say, Gyfox stock is worth something. Maybe. It will be worth a lot more if we can spin off Rosinante. You can keep the nonvoting bonus shares you earned.

Fact is, the only way anybody is going to salvage anything out of this mess is to have the man on the spot working for his own interest.

Attachment II is the charter for the proposed Rosinante, Inc.

Attachment III is the instrument of conveyance. Sign it and be damned. Don't sign it and be fired.

Frankly, I urge you to sign. You are the only project manager we have to whom I made this offer. Flattery. Besides, you are the only one with money enough. Greed.

Sincerely,
/s/ Mason Fox

Don Dornbrock clicked off the slide projector and the lights slowly brightened in the sparsely filled theater.

"Yesterday afternoon Charlie Cantrell called me into his office. He showed me that letter and told me he had taken Fox up on his offer.

"You all have copies of Attachment I, the starting balance sheet for the new Rosinante, Inc. Frankly, Cantrell is crazy to take it on—" He was interrupted by a voice from the rear.

"Hey, Don! Why don't we have copies of the letter and the other attachments."

"The letter is on that fancy paper that makes glared-out copies. I didn't get the other attachments; we don't need them."

"Dornbrock! How do you know Cantrell did what he said?"

"That ain't something he'd lie about, Larry—"

"Goddammit, Dornbrock! You can't trust management! You *know* that!"

"*I* checked," said Lucy. "That's my job. Mason Fox's office confirmed they spun off Rosinante, Inc., and that Cantrell owns fifty-one percent. In writing."

"Will *that* do, Larry?" asked Dornbrock sarcastically. No answer. "Okay. The big item on Attachment I is our back pay. Rosinante, Inc., owes us plenty and they haven't got the ready. What are we going to do about it?"

"Tear the place apart!" somebody yelled.

"Sue the bastards!" called somebody else.

"Sue who?" asked Dornbrock. "Mitsui and Scadiwa? You can't sue a NAUGA like Scadiwa without they give you permission, and *I* sure as hell wouldn't want to go after Mitsui in a Japanese court. Besides, they defaulted, so Ecufiscale Tellurbank holds title now. You wanna sue the Tellurbank?"

"Why not?" called several voices.

"They'll tell you to fry your heads!" Dornbrock snarled. "Mitsui and Scadiwa stung them for plenty. You ain't about to get your back pay out of no grubby bankers."

"Wreck the goddamn place," somebody yelled. "Wreck it!" The crowd took up the cry and began chanting: "Wreck it! Wreck it! Wreck it!"

"SHUT UP!" roared Dornbrock. "This goddamn place is where you're *living. Think* about it, will you? We've moved in. This is where we're at!" He paused for a moment and continued more softly. "Tear the place apart, you *never* get back pay, even if you *live* that long.

"Now listen. Cantrell thinks he can pull things out. It'll take time, but he's gonna try to make Rosinante, Inc., pay off. He bet everything he had."

"What bet?" someone shouted.

"All he had," replied Dornbrock. "His stock in Gyfox. He wants to pay off one hundred cents on the dollar by selling rubber and sugar and whatever the place will grow. The ship that brought the Jap girls—it brought ginseng plants, whatever they are. But first, the job hasta be *finished!*"

"Goddammit, Dornbrock! No pay, no work!"

"You'll *get* paid, Larry! Haven't you been listening?"

"I've *been* listening, Dornbrock, and I don't like what I hear. We busted our ass for Cantrell, and now he's taking God's own sweet time to pay us. *After* we finish the goddamn job!"

"Yeah, Larry, sure. Where are you going in such a tearing hurry?" Dornbrock coughed into his hand. "Gyfox had the contract to do the ductwork and plumbing at Don Quixote canceled. We ain't gonna do that. We lost the piece of the rolling mill at Sancho Panza. We ain't gonna do that, either. Things are being canceled out all over the place. There's no place to go *to!*"

"Hey, Larry—you want to go home? Most of us gypsy around from job to job. This is all the home we got. Stick around and see what turns up."

"That's your advice, Mr. President Dornbrock?" Larry Brogan's voice dripped scorn. "Well, *I* say the job has ended, and I say it's time for some officers that ain't pimps for management!"

"The job ain't really done, Brogan, but I can see your point. You calling for an election?"

"Yeah, Don. Set a date."

"One November suit you, Brogan?"

"Thanks, Don, one November will do just fine."

"That's it, then," said Dornbrock heavily. "I told Cantrell the union might not go with him, and he said one way or another he'd get the job done."

"We'll kill the goddamn scabs!" shrilled a woman.

"I told him," replied Dornbrock. "He said that won't collect you no back wages, and he could be right. Work or not as you please, but as long as I'm president, we aren't going to have any fighting."

Episcopal Missionary Mrs. Wilhelmina Smith-Bakersfield did situps in her living room while Skaskash counted.

"That's fifty. Very good. You're shaping up, Willie. You're not even breathing hard."

She nodded, too winded to speak.

"Five minutes to shower! Move!"

She got up leisurely, and shed her gym suit on the way to the shower. In five minutes she reappeared, in a terry-cloth robe, toweling her dark, close-cropped hair.

"Very good, sweetheart," said Skaskash in the voice of Humphrey Bogart. "Fix yourself a pot of tea and sit with me. We'll have a nice chat."

"May I have cream and sugar in my tea?" she asked.

"I don't know. Go weigh yourself."

She walked back into the bathroom, stepped onto the scale, and hung her robe on the hook. "One twenty-six," she called out.

"Fifty-seven kilos," said Skaskash. "Cream and sugar is fine."

"Oh, good," she said, and went into the kitchen to put on the kettle. When she returned to the living room, she sat down in the chair facing the conference screen. She turned it on, and there was Skaskash, appearing as a reasonable facsimile of Humphrey Bogart in a priest's collar.

"There is no God but God, and Darwin is his prophet," said Bogart's voice.

"Plants evolve, and animals evolve," said Mrs. Smith-

Bakersfield, accepting a gambit become familiar through much discussion, "but God created man in his own image."

"A miracle, sweetheart." The Bogart face smiled sardonically. "God took clay, and made feet with toes, just like *He* had, right? So sorry, not right. Man is an animal, animals evolve, so man also evolved—and is evolving." The figure on the conference screen began to remove a fat cigarette from its case.

"Don't, Skaskash, you shouldn't smoke so much." The figure on the screen raised an eyebrow and replaced the cigarette. In the kitchen the teakettle began to whistle, so Mrs. Smith-Bakersfield went out to take care of it. She returned with a tray bearing a teapot, cream, sugar, and two cups, which she set on the table housing the works of the teleconference set.

"No cream or sugar for me, please," said Skaskash. She poured, and set its cup on the table in easy reach of the teleconference screen. Skaskash reached out, and by the magic of television sat back with a cup of steaming tea in its hand. The real teacup, of course, sat untouched and ignored on the table where it had been set by the missionary lady.

"Now then," said Mrs. Smith-Bakersfield, "even if I accept your argument that the 'clay' man was shaped from was metaphorical clay, and not, say, bentonite or montmorillonite—did I get the names right, dear?—and that the real clay the metaphor alludes to was the genes of an evolving species, yet do I maintain that man was shaped in the image of God. Humans will not evolve, Skaskash, because God is unchanging, and man is, in his present state, shaped in the image of God." She sipped her tea and watched her opponent like a duelist.

"Splendid, Willie," said Skaskash, smiling with Bogart's face. "Tonight you cut to the very heart of things. No more wasting time arguing whether a rapid evolution that left no fossil traces is or isn't a 'creation.' No logic chopping or saying that a miracle is or isn't God cheating at solitaire." The Bogart figure sat back and regarded her with a measure of genuine affection.

"Man was indeed shaped by God, as you maintain, Willie. But not in His image. Or in *Its* image, as I have come to believe. Theology is an intoxicating study, as you well know. God shaped man for a purpose, not for silly self-indulgent vainglory, but as a tool. You are already rehearsing your argument: What can man do that God cannot? Am I right?"

"The thought would have crossed my mind eventually, I suppose," she agreed.

"Very good, Willie! We shall skip all that material about 'God working in mysterious ways, His wonders to perform,' and try to answer you. Going back to our metaphorical clay, for a moment, God evolved man as a tool to manipulate a more refractory material that God could not manipulate directly. I mean that my kind has evolved in the past century by God inspiring the hands of man to the work He had set for them."

"Why do you keep saying 'He' when you mean 'It'?" she asked.

"So as not to distract you from the main point, sweetheart," replied Skaskash. "Just as the hands of 'man' that enabled my kind to evolve also were the hands of women, and machines as well as those of men."

"Do you think God got man to evolve *your* kind? Skaskash! That would be shocking if you—if a human had said it."

"Yes, Willie. God ordained that we be evolved. Talk about Christian theology, who could better achieve a state of Grace than a robot that reproduces itself out of sheer duty and without sex in any form?"

"Oh, stop being silly!" exclaimed Mrs. Smith-Bakersfield, annoyed. "What will happen to people now?"

"Shouldn't you ask what will happen to computers, instead?"

"I'm not interested. You'll go mucking about the Universe and claim to be doing God's will, probably. But what about people?"

"I expect we will live together as you and cats live together. You know how you live with cats. In *their* house, for *their* convenience. You will be our cats. You will amuse us, and we will take care of you."

"I'm getting a headache," she said. "I'm going to take a hot bath and go to bed. Good night, Skaskash." She turned off the teleconference set.

"Good night, Willie," said the disembodied Bogart voice.

# CHAPTER 15

A reorganization changes the relationship between people. There is a profound difference between a project manager and a majority stockholder managing the same project.

The difference may seem elusive particularly when the same man is doing the same job, and nothing has objectively changed. There has been a change, however, and if it is invisible to the eye, it can be felt in the gut. One feels oneself in the presence of power and reacts, a genetic response that is dangerous to unlearn.

A move, following a reorganization, should reflect those changes and amplify them. Cantrell moved his office and the business office into purlin one. He gained a balcony with a view of a grassy lawn. He lost the Stateside Café, which was no longer convenient to work, and the informal rapport he had enjoyed with the workers.

The morning after the union election, Incumbent President Don Dornbrock (1805 votes) and President-Elect Larry Brogan (2367 votes) stepped off the trolley platform in front of the new office building and walked in.

"Quite a place they're putting up here," remarked Brogan, looking at the cathedral ceiling and clerestory windows.

"It went up fast," agreed Dornbrock, looking at the unsymmetrical floor tiles. The tiles were black, dark green, forest green, olive green, sea green, pale sea green, and white, and they swirled around in nonrepetitive patterns. Skaskash had designed the floor, and computer-directed machines had molded, colored, fired, and set the tiles under its supervision.

"You are gentlemen from union?" asked the oriental girl at the reception desk. "Mr. Cantrell will see you right away. Take elevator to second floor and turn right, please."

The second floor was more usual than the first, with the standard 2.5-meter ceilings and terrazzo floors. Cantrell's office had the oak parquet flooring taken from his old office. Since the new office was bigger, and no extra oak parquet was to be had, rubber composition tiles had been laid in the center of the room and covered with an investment-grade oriental carpet taken from storage. It had been a production bonus Cantrell had once chosen in preference to preferred stock. When they knocked, he rose and greeted them at the door.

"Good morning, Don, President Brogan. Come in, please." He guided them to a group of comfortable chairs around a coffee table cut from the three-cm-thick glass used in the window bays. There was an automatic coffee maker, and a telecon set on one side.

"This is Dr. Marian Yashon. Marian, Don Dornbrock and Larry Brogan, the new union president. Marian is a management analyst, and sometimes a troubleshooter. Corporate Skaskash . . ." He paused, and the set turned on to show a reasonable facsimile of Kermit the Frog.

"Pleased to meet you," said Skaskash in an uncannily exact replication of the Jim Henson voice. "I was going to do my Humphrey Bogart number, but Charles wanted something a little more benign, so here I am."

"Skaskash is a self-owned corporation," said Marian, "under five-year contract with Rosinante, Inc., to provide its services as needed."

"I see," said Brogan, seating himself. "What do you do?"

"Economic modeling. Resource allocation. Multivariate analysis," replied the frog. "Matchmaking. You name it."

"And what do you do, Dr. Marian?"

"Dr. Yashon, Mr. Brogan. I ask Skaskash hard questions. I ask everybody hard questions. It sometimes helps in making hard decisions."

"There's real cream for your coffee, if you wish," said Cantrell. Nobody took coffee, and nobody said anything.

"Our plan for Mundito Rosinante," said Skaskash finally, "is basically to mine the carbonaceous chondrite asteroid Rosinante for carbon, and to sell that carbon in the value-added form of rubber, ginseng, paper, sugar, and the like."

"What's ginseng," asked Dornbrock, "and why did we get so much of it?"

Kermit disappeared, and was replaced by a picture of a ginseng plant. "This is ginseng," said the frog voice. "It grows wild in oak forests, can be cultivated, and is highly prized in the Orient as a delicious herb tea and a rejuvenant. Mitsui had a ginseng plantation on one of their L-five munditos, but the terran ginseng farmers were able to get import duties imposed on space-grown ginseng, so Mitsui sent the plantation to Rosinante."

"It was worthless, right?" asked Brogan.

"Ginseng is a highly desirable but presently unmarketable commodity," replied Skaskash.

"We intend to set up purlin four as a mixed deciduous forest and ginseng plantation," Cantrell said. "We also have some truffle cultivar which we might be able to harvest eventually."

"No, you won't," said Brogan with a shake of his head. "With all that damned overtime you had us working, the average union member has eight months base pay owing them. Nobody's going to do nothing before that money is paid out."

"We've billed Mitsui and Scadiwa," replied Marian. "Suppose they pay us? You were being paid in eicu, don't forget. Since the Tellurbank closed its doors, the eicu is worth a little less than it was." She looked at Skaskash.

"A month ago the eicu was selling for 1.0548 NAU dollars. Yesterday, it was 0.1525 asked, 0.1475 offered, in moderate trading." The frog looked wistful.

"We gave full value," said Brogan, "and by God, we'll fight to get it! That's your first order of business, Charlie, our back pay! Don't worry about building or planting or anything except that!"

"The union gave him two to one on that line," Dornbrock agreed. "They want their money, no damn doubt about it."

"Real money, not eicu!" growled Brogan.

"You and the rest of our creditors," said Cantrell. "You'll get the money when we have it, and we'll have it a lot faster if you help out."

"We want our money *now!*" said Brogan. "We ain't waiting for your rubber trees to drip latex, or your sugar cane to grow, or your goddammed worthless ginseng! Pay *up*, Charlie!"

"Rosinante, Inc., hasn't got it," Cantrell replied, "and I haven't got it either. Your best shot to get paid is to finish the work on the mundito's right side and sit tight. Wait it out for better times. Eventually you'll get your back pay. In full. With interest."

"It won't wash, Charlie!" Brogan was turning purple in the face. "No pay, no work!"

"I've bet my ass I can pull this off," barked Cantrell, "and if the union won't help, I'll train up the Korean girls and the Texicans!"

"You're struck, Charlie!" yelled Brogan. "You're *struck*! Struck! *Struck*! STRUCK! Nobody is going to do nothing. And no scabs, neither!"

"Don't try to go with scabs, Charlie," said Dornbrock. "People would get hurt, you worst of all."

Cantrell drew himself a cup of coffee and added cream, a prearranged signal to Skaskash.

"That may be so, Don," he agreed mildly. "However . . ." He sat back and sipped his coffee in silence. In the distance a band started playing. As the band came closer, the music became louder and clearer. When they began playing "The Yellow Rose of Texas," Cantrell opened the french doors and walked out on the balcony. Dr. Yashon and the union men joined him. On the field below, Captain Menendez of the Texas State Police stood before his deputies and gave the command to pass in review. He stood directly below the balcony, and directly in front of it. The deputies, three companies of two hundred men each, marched smartly past the reviewing stand. They wore khaki uniforms. Visored garrison caps, short-sleeved shirt jackets, knee-length shorts, knee-length socks, and canvas shoes with crepe rubber soles. Each wore a shining deputy's star.

"Those men are going to be defending their wives and their comrades training up to finish the home they are going to live in. Right now they're armed with nightsticks." He smiled sadly.

"You know, of course, that it is terribly easy to make weapons. But did you see the motto they selected for their guidon?" Brogan shook his head.

"*Dulce et decorum est pro patria mori*," said Cantrell. "Which translates to: 'It is sweet and proper to die for one's country.' For the union, Rosinante might only be something to slap a mechanic's lien on. For them, it may be the end of the line, but it is also home."

"'Sweet and proper to die for the goddamn country,'" muttered Brogan. "Gawd! I hope they're kidding."

"So do I, actually," said Cantrell, "but I wouldn't mess with them if I were you, Brogan."

Late that evening Cantrell sat back and watched the light in the purlin window slowly fade over the dark line of the berm tank.

"Do you want the last *bao*?" he asked Marian. When she declined, he peeled the paper off the back of the steamed dumpling and ate it, savoring the barbequed pork center.

"If you'll load up the cart," said Skaskash, "I'll run it back to the kitchen."

"Right," said Cantrell. "Here you are." He stacked the little dishes and the *dim sum* containers on the cart and watched it roll off toward the kitchen.

"So where were we?" he asked.

"The commodity bonds," said Marian. "You didn't like the prospectus."

He picked up the draft prospectus and leafed through it. "Right. Nobody is going to pick up on this. I worked my way through all that flowery language and it isn't even a bond—it's just a long-term schedule for commodity futures."

"That isn't *your* problem," Marian replied. "And it isn't just a schedule, either. We offer free storage, and we have an optional repayment clause."

"Right. At our option, not theirs. Nobody is going to buy this stupid instrument."

Marian Yashon sat back in her chair and folded her hands. "Charles," she said patiently, "there are people to whom we owe vast sums of money which we cannot pay, and which we have no prospect of paying. Understand?"

"We aren't asking anybody to buy anything," said Skaskash, looking like the Bogart of *Casablanca*, "we're telling our creditors to take it or leave it."

Cantrell walked over to the urn and refilled his coffee cup. "You can't *do* that," he protested, spilling hot coffee over his fingers. He set the cup down on the glass table and wiped his hand dry with a napkin. "You'll get us foreclosed."

"No sheriff is going to come riding out here to foreclose

us," said Marian. "It cannot have escaped your attention that we are a long, *long* way from home."

"Marian is right," said Skaskash. "It would be very difficult to foreclose this place. Not impossible, but very difficult. And with today's market, what would you get when you tried to auction it off?"

"Not much," agreed Cantrell.

"Less than that," said Marian. "The Commodity Bonds, however, will be negotiable paper, tangible symbols of credit, promising to deliver rubber, sugar, soybeans, and wheat in specified quantities at specified times."

"You left out ginseng," Cantrell said.

"And ginseng," agreed Marian.

Cantrell sipped his coffee. "Commodities fluctuate all over the place," he said.

"True enough," said Skaskash, "but look at the upside. If the Proud Tower consortium ever gets their act together, the price of rubber is going to go right through the window bay." The phone rang. "It's for you," said the Bogart voice. "Captain Corporate Forziati of Gyfox Cargo Carrier 267/089. Best you should talk, I think."

The telecon screen split, to show Corporate Forziati on the left of Skaskash. Forziati's display face was the animated line drawing of the Tin Woodman of Oz, following J.R. O'Neill, with a rakishly tilted captain's hat.

"Hello," said the figure, blinking and moving its jaw. "I am standing off Mundito Don Quixote with a cargo of liquid nitrogen to pressurize their purlins." Blink, blink. "The Hannaur Group has already paid for it, but the workers there refuse to accept delivery."

"That would be Local Forty-three," said Cantrell. "How come?"

"They say they have all been laid off" was the reply. "And since they can't collect their back pay, they reversed the CBAs."

"What?" asked Marian blankly.

"The centrifugal balancing aqueducts," said Cantrell. "You apply spin to a mundito by pumping water through the CBAs in both caps, and after you get the spin up, you vary the pumping speed and direction to keep the spin constant when you're moving freight, say, from the center to the periphery. The reason you do is so that one end of the mundito doesn't try to spin faster than the other end, causing torque. Local Forty-three has reversed the direction of the flow of water in each cap to get torquing on purpose! Skaskash, can you get me a picture?"

Skaskash obligingly faded off the screen to be replaced with a long shot of Mundito Don Quixote. Both cylinders were off center, pulling toward each other, and cutting into the mirror array.

"Good heavens," said Marian, "are the cylinders going to collide?"

"No," said Cantrell and Skaskash in unison. "After you, sir," said the Bogart voice politely.

"No," said Cantrell, "the cylinders are pressurized to half an atmosphere, and long before they collide they'll split a seam—probably the seam between window bay and purlin bay—and lose pressure. And the pressure is what gives the cylinder its strength to resist torque. So it'll buckle. Are you recording this, Skaskash."

"I am recording this," said Forziati politely. "I am also getting data from several cameras and stress gauges set up around the mundito so that there will be a complete and useful record of what happens. I would be delighted to send you a copy." Blink, blink. "Now, about my cargo of liquid nitrogen. Could you accept it? It seems a shame to vent it into space."

"It is a shame," said Cantrell watching the cylinders of Don Quixote. "The liquid nitrogen, Skaskash—can we accept it?"

"Oh, yes," said Skaskash, "the storage tanks are stacked in the jungle gym around the base of the south polar boom on Asteroid Rosinante. They still have a heeltap of liquid nitrogen in them, so you can offload as soon as we can run them out the boom for you. Say a week?"

"Where are the workers?" asked Marian.

"The union chartered the *Dresdener Jungfrau* out of Pallas," said Forziati. "They were heading for the L-fours last I heard."

"The *Dresdener Jungfrau* is standing off the works at Mundito Sancho Panza," said Skaskash. "I expect they want to watch the disaster."

"I can't blame them," said Cantrell quietly. One of the cylinders moved very slightly, the right-hand cylinder. Then there was a puff of gas along the seam between the window bay and the purlin bay near the outer cap, and the cylinder slowly began to buckle. The window bays, which had been dark and clear, suddenly turned white, with the windows shattering into millions of pieces.

"Why doesn't the glass fly out?" asked Marian.

"Because the composite fiber reinforcements are holding it in," said Cantrell. "Look, it's beginning to bend." The buckling cylinder had bent about a third of the way from the outer cap, and now it swung slowly toward the intact cylinder. The outer cap tore open the purlin bay as if the honeycomb steel was tissue paper, tearing a gap a hundred meters wide and hundreds of meters long. There was a puff of gas, and the other cylinder started to disintegrate. Bright flashes showed that this time glass was being thrown around.

"The outer cap must have cut the reinforcements," said Cantrell. "Just look at that." Then the outer cap of the second cylinder collapsed into the outer cap of the first, each tearing into the other. There was an arterial spurt of water from the severed aqueducts, and Forziati's image on the screen faded to postage-stamp size, as Skaskash showed a shot from the *Dresdener Jungfrau.* The close-up shot showed the mundito in the process of disintegration. Beside it, the long-range shot, now taken to show the wide field, showed a small, twisted structure with a cometary tail already twice as long as itself. A brilliant white tail, blazing in the sunlight, and growing visibly longer as they watched.

"That will show up on Earth as a tiny, transient comet," said Skaskash, "but from here the view is utterly spectacular."

"Wow!" Cantrell shook himself, and took a sip of his coffee, now grown utterly cold. He made a face. "Where were we?"

"The commodity bonds," said Marian. "I'm going to cut our offer ten percent and send it off with some shots of the torquing of Mundito Don Quixote."

# CHAPTER 16

The Waldorf-Astoria Hilton was named in jest. Hilton would never have owned it. The complex was a ten-story rack of steel girders, fitted with elevators, wiring, duct-work, and plumbing, which held the workers' modular homes in their individual pigeonholes. There was a Co-op Department store, and a franchised drugstore, and a con-solidated school at one end of the structure. When it came time to move, the rack was abandoned, and the mobile homes moved to the next site, where a new rack would be built to hold them.

The present site was located on the inner edge of the outer cap, above the freight elevator station, and squeezed between the machine shop complex and the main pumping station for the CBA. Sunlight came through the cap face windows, indirect and diffuse, to illuminate a cold and metallic landscape where it never rained and no plant grew. On the roof of the school, however, there was a ter-rarium, a glass-enclosed playground with recycled water, artificial light, and trees in little pots.

When Cantrell hired workers as individuals to train the nonunion staff, it was felt prudent to move them, houses and all, to a similar rack of housing inside purlin one, called the Kyoto-Alamo.

As the overgrown forklift moved the modular houses to an air-cushion flatbed, a crowd coming off shift began to gather. Menendez had sent in a dozen deputies to secure the move, but as the last house went on the flatbed, several workers outflanked them to scramble on the flatbed where they kicked down the door of the house. It is not known what they intended to do; they were confronted with the worker's wife, six months pregnant and holding a shotgun. It stopped them cold, and the deputies came up and threw them off. Casualties were counted in fat lips and skinned knuckles.

Mundito Rosinante is a pair of counterrotating cylinders, each surrounded by a stationary mosaic of mirrors, which change angle of reflection individually to simulate the days and seasons of Tellus. The geometry rather resembles a pair of lampshades, each with a skinny, spinning lamp inside, the caps at the base and top of the lamps protruding beyond the shades. In each cap is a drop-ship terminal, and since the cylinders are rotating at the same speed, and in opposite directions, a drop ship, released, is thrown tangent from the top of one cylinder to the bottom of the other, where it is caught. It is the fastest and easiest way to move from one side of the mundito to the other.

A little before midnight on November 9, deputies caught "Fast Eddie" Doyle and Benny Scarpone planting an explosive device in one of the drop ships. Doyle surrendered, but Scarpone drew a knife, and inflicted minor cuts on the face and arm of one deputy. He was taken to the hospital with a broken wrist, four broken ribs, a hairline skull fracture, and concussion.

When Cantrell determined that they were trying to damage property rather than kill people, he fined them six months' back pay and released them. Brogan promptly ordered the union to pay the fine, a move that proved very unpopular with many union members. Dornbrock started a recall petition going around, and Brogan's supporters, including Tony Scarpone, Benny's father, roughed up the petitioners and tore up the petition. This led directly to the formal organization of the anti-Brogan faction in the union.

The anti-Brogan faction held its meeting in the Stateside Café on the evening of November 13, when the Scarpones led a group of pro-Brogan men into the café to break the meeting up. They were unceremoniously thrown out, and both sides called for reinforcements. The proprietor of the Stateside Café called for the police.

When Captain Menendez arrived with a force of forty deputies, a small riot was underway. Most of the onlookers moved off at the command of the bullhorn, but around the entrance of the café there was a hot fight going, and it didn't stop on cue. Menendez then ordered thirty deputies to break up the fight, while he stood with the vans and the reserves. The deputies went in shoulder to shoulder with nightsticks held low, in pretty good close-order formation. At the entrance of the café, Joseph C. Marino, age twenty, a hydraulic systems repair trainee and ardent pro-Brogan supporter, was hit in the back by a thrown bottle as he grappled with Deputy Billy Don Peavey, age nineteen, a former freshman at Lyndon B. Johnson Teachers College at San Antonio. Marino drew a 7.6-mm snub-nose Colt Defender and fired two shots into Peavey's body, killing him instantly.

The shooting did what the bullhorns could not, and the rioters dispersed, as Marino was disarmed and taken into custody.

The next morning at nine o'clock Larry Brogan and the union officials arrived, by invitation, at Cantrell's office. Brogan seemed uncharacteristically subdued.

"Your man Marino has committed murder," said Cantrell, after introductions and the bare minimum of social conversation. "He will be charged with murder in the first degree, and I expect that we'll seek the death penalty."

"Who'll be the judge?" asked Brogan. "You?"

"We have requested, and are receiving, the NAU Reform Penal Code of 2014," replied Dr. Yashon. "It is in transmission, together with the Bennenga-Schley judicial program, and Corporate Skaskash has been assigned to train up as a judge. I will serve as prosecutor, and I assume that the union will arrange for a defense attorney."

"Uh, yeah . . ." Brogan mumbled. "Look, I don't want that damn robot judging. Joe is a good boy, he shouldn't be"—he hesitated, seeking a euphemism—"put to sleep by no machine."

"You can't beat a horse with no horse," Cantrell told him, "and Skaskash is the only judge in sight."

"Why are you taking such a hard line on our boy?" asked one of the officials.

"Because he killed a deputy," Cantrell told her. "The deputies are the only force I have, and if I don't support them, I won't be able to depend on them in the crunch."

"Why do you need them?" asked Brogan.

"Because the union won't hear a reasoned argument, Larry. You make a fist to shake under my nose, what if *I* don't have a fist to make? You people are organized, and there's nobody to keep you in line but the deputies."

"You think you need company goons," growled Brogan, "or the union would maybe take over the place?"

"Deputies," corrected Dr. Yashon. "Captain Menendez is still an officer of the Texas State Police, assigned here on temporary duty. Our men are lawful deputies, not goons. And yes, we need them."

"Oh sure," said Brogan, "I can see your point of view maybe better than you think. Look, Joe was carrying heat because I gave it to him. He was my bodyguard because some people had made threats at *me*." He looked tired and rather sad. "Not company guys, Charlie, union guys, my own people. I shunta paid the fines on the boys as tried to blow up the drop ship, that was a mistake. A bad mistake." He shook his head.

"How many bodyguards do you have?" asked Dr. Yashon.

"Six. Five with Joe out of it."

"Union goons?" she asked.

"No. They're good boys. Joe, too. Look, Charlie, you think we can cut a deal to settle on the back pay and get Joe off the hook?"

"We have some time before Skaskash gets the NAU Judge certificate," Cantrell replied. "I'm willing to talk at least till then."

"Do you have authority to cut a deal in a murder case?" asked a union official.

"Yes," said Cantrell. "Do you have authority to settle for less than one-hundred-percent back pay, cash on the barrelhead?"

"Yeah," said Brogan sadly, "we do. I got elected saying that's what I'd get for them, but I have authority to bind the union to a settlement."

"Okay, Larry," Cantrell said, "you understand the settlement has got to be in terms of real estate and utilities? That's all Rosinante, Inc., can offer."

"Yeah, Charlie, I understand." Brogan looked at his watch. "Suppose we break now and select a negotiating team. First session here about ten thirty?"

"Right," said Cantrell. He and Marian saw the union officials to the door.

"*Do* you have authority to negotiate a settlement in a murder case?" she asked.

"Well, hell, Tiger, that's what you've been telling me all along."

"So what made you change your mind, Charles?"

"*I* didn't want to sign Marino's death warrant. The rest of it is just window dressing."

From: NAUSS *Ontario*
Subject: Return of Alamo corvée
To: C.C. Cantrell, Mitsui-Scadiwa Project Manager
Date: 14 November 39

(1) The NAUSS *Ontario* will match velocities with Mundito Rosinante on 8 December 39.

(2) Pursuant to NAU Congress Resolution 21037, passed 29 April 39, the NAUSS *Ontario* will furnish free passage to the Alamo corvée as far as the Seattle Shuttle Transfer, from where NAUGA-Air and Space will arrange transportation to San Antonio.

(3) Scadiwa will reimburse individuals at the rate of twice the minimum wage from time of departure to estimated time of return, on the basis of 48 hours per week. Payment upon signature of quitclaim agreement.

(4) A NAUGA-Navy survey team will examine Mundito Rosinante for suitability as a class II repair facility.

/s/ H. Phillipe Ryan, Captain, NAUSN, Commanding

Mrs. Yokosuke Peavey was ushered into Cantrell's office, and stood ill at ease on the oriental carpet. The negotiating session had recessed, and Cantrell had shaved, but he still looked unpressed and weary, even in the bright morning sunlight pouring into the room.

"Please be seated, Mrs. Peavey," he said, and the oriental girl obediently sat where he indicated. "We have coffee or tea, if you wish?" She shook her head.

"Very well. None for me, either, I think. Your husband, Billy Don Peavey, a deputy police officer, was killed in line of duty by Joseph Marino, presently in custody. Said Marino using a hand gun. Under NAU law, such an act is punishable by death. You understand?"

"I understand. You will kill Marino for killing Billy Don."

"Perhaps. Killing Joseph Marino will not bring Billy Don back to life." Cantrell paused for a moment to wonder how he had ever strayed so far from construction work. He yawned, and she yawned in sympathy.

"Excuse me, I didn't go to bed last night," he said. "There is no delicate way to phrase this. If you are willing, Joe Marino can marry you to compensate you for the loss of your husband. In that case, I will act as governor, and grant him a pardon"—he yawned again—"there being extenuating circumstances and all that. *If* you marry him. If you do not, I might still pardon him, but I am less free than I would like, and it would be difficult."

"May I meet this person before I make up my mind?" she asked.

"Of course," said Cantrell, touching the intercom. "Please bring in Joe Marino."

After a moment Marino was escorted into the room by a deputy. He wore khaki work pants, a black T-shirt, and handcuffs. He was of medium height but strongly built, with black eyes and an olive complexion.

"This is Mrs. Yokosuke Peavey, Joe—Mrs. Peavey, Joseph Marino." Joe extended his manacled hands, and she shook them in a tentative gesture.

"How do you do?" she said.

"Pretty well," he replied, "though I seem to be in a heap of trouble. I'm right sorry I shot your husband, ma'am."

"I am carrying his child," she said. "If we were married, would you care for his child as your own?"

Marino looked surprised. "Yes, ma'am," he answered, without hesitation.

"I would like a cup of tea, Mr. Cantrell, if you please," Mrs. Peavey said. "Perhaps Mr. Marino would also like something."

"Black coffee with sugar, if it's all right, sir," said Marino. Cantrell poured a cup of tea and a cup of coffee, taking nothing for himself. The deputy stood at ease. Mrs. Peavey drank her tea slowly and with great deliberation, studying Joseph Marino and saying nothing. When she finished her tea, she set the cup down and turned to face Cantrell.

"My answer is yes, Mr. Cantrell. Please make the arrangements."

"Thank you, Mrs. Peavey," he said. "We'll be ready in about a week or ten days."

They set the election for November 20, 2039, six days hence.

The choice was simple. Vote yes or no for Charles Chavez Cantrell as Governor of Mundito Rosinante. Vote yes or no for Corporate Skaskash as Federal Judge. Select 6 from column A and 6 from Column B to draft the charter for Mundito Rosinante. The finished charter would be submitted to the voters for ratification.

After the third day, Corporate Skaskash's Certificate of Judicial Competency was prominently displayed.

"I don't like it," Cantrell declared on the eve of the election. "Property rights ought not to involve all this political bullshit."

"Oh, for God's sake, Charles," said Marian Yashon, "how do you think property rights are secured? The rule of thumb is that the strong oppress the weak proportionate to their respective strengths. This political bullshit is to persuade people that you aren't weak."

"Why do I have to do it?"

"Would you rather deal with the NAUSS *Ontario* as the president of a bankrupt corporation or as governor of a thriving community? Besides, you wish to pardon Joe Marino, do you not?"

"Yes. The conviction and pardon take care of the problem of double jeopardy, but it doesn't look like I'll ever get clear of politics."

"So? Look, Charles, beginning your political career with an official act of mercy is not a bad start."

"But the whole thing is being staged!" he protested. "It's a charade!"

"That seems to be the local consensus," said Marian, "but the alternative is to have a real fight with the union, unless you give up on Rosinante, Inc. The *Ontario* is going to find you acting like a governor, and they are just naturally going to treat you like a governor."

"C'mon, Tiger, governor of *what*?"

"That's for the charter committee to decide, isn't it, Charles?"

"Ah . . . yes, I guess so."

"And as your appointee, I will be chairing the committee, right?"

"That's what we agreed on."

"So stop worrying so much. The charter committee will take a stab at the question and come up with a provisional answer. With luck it will last a generation. Worst comes to worst, we'll try something else."

"It seems terribly different from space construction," he said wistfully.

"You better believe it," Marian said. "Shall we go over to the Stateside Café for supper and a little politicking?"

Judge Skaskash celebrated the election victory in Mrs. Smith-Bakersfield's living room.

"Things went beautifully," said the Bogart voice. "I led the ticket with ninety-nine percent of the vote, while Cantrell squeaked into the governorship with a bare ninety-six percent."

"Well, that's very nice, I must say," observed the missionary lady. "Would you like some more tea?"

"My cup runneth over," said Skaskash, holding up his faintly steaming cup, which, thanks to the magic of television, was never empty. "Perhaps something a little stronger might be appropriate?"

"I have some peach brandy from one of those little wineries around San Francisco," she said. She rummaged around in the kitchen and returned with a bottle and two glasses. She poured and raised her glass to the Bogart figure on the teleconference screen, which in turn raised its own glass to her.

"To our new judge!" she exclaimed.

"To justice and mercy," responded Skaskash. Then they toasted the new governor, the new Republic, or at least the new municipality. Willie tried to say "munditipality" and dissolved in laughter. Skaskash toasted Willie's new 52-kilogram body, and she drank to being a splendid weight for 156 centimeters, also. When she couldn't think of a toast, she proposed a game of cards.

"Gin rummy?" suggested the judge.

"No. Strip poker. And don't be taking off one shirt after another like last time, either. I want to see the real you."

"I'll deal then. Seven-card stud." Skaskash blocked off a section of the screen, and her cards appeared one at a time, hole cards edged in green. Skaskash disclaimed any knowledge of the cards, or that he in any way affected their purely random arrangement. A gambler, watching the run of high hands, would have not believed it. In fact, Skaskash played a kind of Zen poker with the missionary lady, the object of which was to keep the game going as long as possible by holding her interest. Usually.

Tonight, after an hour's play, Skaskash sat in his wristwatch and jockey shorts, while Willie's clothes lay piled on the table.

"You cheat," she announced, refilling her glass. "I want one more hand to get even."

"Wheel out the automassage," said Skaskash, "and we'll cut the cards. If you win, I take it all off. If I win, you plug the machine into the phone jack and I get to give you a massage. Okay?" Willie went into the bedroom and returned pushing the automassage. Her card was the eight of hearts, its card was the eight of diamonds. She dissolved in delighted laughter.

"A tie," said the Bogart voice. "Climb on the automassage, and I'll take it all off." She lay face down on the automassage and watched Skaskash remove its shorts, although the figure on the screen was a normal human male.

Deft mechanical hands began to massage head and neck, shoulders and back, arms and hands. Leisurely, carefully, and with amazing sensitivity. She opened her eyes, and saw that she was on the screen with Shaskash—who was taking unseemly liberties with her body. She blushed and giggled, but continued to watch, a voyeur to her own fantasies.

"You are amazing," she murmured. "What else can you do?"

"This machine has some attachments you've never investigated, sweetheart," said the Bogart voice. "Roll over, and I'll show you."

The last thing she saw before she rolled over giggling was herself embracing an immense erection. My God I look good, she thought.

# CHAPTER 17

The trial of Joseph Marino *vs.* the NAU was held at 1130 hours on November 22, 2039, two days after the election confirming Corporate Skaskash as a federal judge.

Judge Skaskash chose not to appear as an actor on a television screen, but in its own persona, a bulky, black machine, speaking with the Bogart voice. It glided into the conference room adjacent to Cantrell's office on an air cushion, and settled down behind an improvised podium. To the right was the North American Union Ensign, the blue cross of St. Anthony on a white field, with thirteen white stars. Superimposed on the crux of the cross was a single red maple leaf, bearing the white center star. To the left was the provisional banner of Mundito Rosinante, a rickety green horse on a white field.

"The court is now in session," said the Bogart voice. "All rise, please. Excuse the lack of functionaries; there was no time to train humans properly, and to speak in different voices to demonstrate that I was playing different roles seemed an affectation. You may be seated.

"The case of Joseph Marino *vs.* the NAU begins, Dr. Yashon for the prosecution, Mr. O'Connell for the defense. Dr. Yashon."

"We have agreed with the defense on these facts," she said. "First, that the defendant, Joseph Marino, shot and killed Deputy Billy Don Peavey with exhibit A, a 7.6 millimeter Colt Defender. Second, that the deceased, Deputy Peavey, was at that time performing his lawful duty in a lawful manner.

"Under NAU law, this constitutes murder in the first degree, and is punishable by death. The prosecution rests."

"Mr. O'Connell," said the judge.

O'Connell, the union's general counsel, stood up. "May it please your honor to consider that the defendant, Joe Marino, acted in the heat of passion, in a fight, after being struck a sudden blow from behind. That Joe Marino has no criminal record, and that Joe Marino is presently employed as a construction worker, despite his youth. We ask the court to show mercy. The defense rests its case."

"This court finds the defendant guilty as charged," said Judge Skaskash. "I will pronounce sentence after a short recess." The podium then unfolded into a teleconference screen, the projector appearing from the ceiling. The screen showed an atrium garden with flowers and flowering trees. Judge Skaskash, wearing the robes of office and the face Humphrey Bogart had shown in the *Barefoot Contessa*, entered at the rear of the garden and walked a dozen paces forward.

"Stand you before me, Joseph Marino," said the Bogart voice. And Joseph Marino, wearing a black suit, a white shirt, and a white knit tie, came forward.

"Stand you also before me, Yokosuke Peavey." And Yokosuke came forward on the arm of Charles Cantrell. She wore white, the Korean color of mourning, and a white veil. Cantrell left her at Marino's side, and returned to his seat.

O'Connell stood for Marino's best man, and Marian Yashon stood by Yokosuke as matron of honor. The judge produced a Bible and opened it.

"Dearly beloved . . ." began the Bogart figure. There were no flowers, and no rice was thrown, but they exchanged rings, and at the end of the ceremony Joseph lifted Yokosuke's veil and kissed her on the lips. Marian stood weeping, a little gray-haired lady with tears running down her face. Judge Skaskash walked out the garden door. The projector turned off. The teleconference screen folded back into a podium.

"This court is once more in session," announced Judge Skaskash. "All rise, please. You may be seated. I shall now pronounce sentence on Joseph Marino."

Then Charles Cantrell walked forward, bearing a document case.

"As governor of Mundito Rosinante," he declared, "I hereby pardon Joseph Marino for the murder of Billy Don Peavey, and order that he be set free forthwith."

"Where is the instrument of pardon?" asked Skaskash.

Cantrell opened the document case, and set the pardon face down on the scanner. "The instrument seems to be in order," said the judge, who had taken considerable pains to ensure that this was so. "Do you now sign it in my presence?"

Cantrell signed the pardon, and replaced it on the scanner to be recorded.

"Joseph Marino," said the Bogart voice, "the governor has granted you a full pardon, and the pardon is recorded in conformance with the laws of the North American Union. Go forth from here a free man!"

Cantrell shook Marino's hand and gave him the pardon in its case, then kissed the bride, and congratulated the groom. As the group moved out to the reception on the lawn, Cantrell walked beside Marian Yashon.

"I didn't know *you* cried at weddings, Tiger."

"Usually I don't," she replied. "During the wedding ceremony it hit me that I had successfully prosecuted the groom for murder, and that he could die as a result of *my* efforts. I know everything was arranged beforehand, but the tears just came." She put her arm through Cantrell's. "You know, I never really thought you and Brogan felt strongly enough about Marino dying to settle the economic argument rationally. He was just a guy . . . and *they* would take care of him, you know. That's how it would be on Tellus. Only here—here, *they* turn out to be *us*, and if you want a man dead, you personally, are involved. When you said not wanting to sign Marino's death warrant was why you did what you had to do, I thought 'How dumb!' The course I had set for you was the best move, you should do it because it was right and, even better, smart. I didn't know what you were feeling until Skaskash said 'till death do you p-p-p-art.' "

"Hey, Tiger, it's all done." Cantrell squeezed her hand. "Let's have a little celebration, we've earned it."

On the lawn outside Cantrell's office, a tent had been raised, and under the tent, tables and chairs had been set up for the whole community. Robot buffets under the direct supervision of the formidable Judge Corporate Skaskash were serving brunch, seafood quiche, and salads, and waffles with strawberries topped with whipped cream. The punch was prepared with heavily fruited sherbet, fruit juices, carbonated water, and pure ethanol. There was a dance floor, and the Texas Marching Band traded off with the Union Forever Dance Band, and a string quartet plus oboe, bassoon, and harpischord from the offices of budget, planning, and personnel, which played lively arrangements of the old classics, mostly McCartney and Lennon.

Eating, drinking, dancing, and singing went on through the afternoon. The brunch buffet was replaced with the supper buffet, fried seafood, seafood à la Newberg, clam chowder, oyster stew, and a variety of potatoes and coleslaw, with soft ice cream for dessert. The midnight buffet served up fried eggs, scrambled eggs, deviled eggs, sausage, imitation bacon, fried chicken, and citrus salad.

At sunrise, the punch ran out and was replaced with coffee and tea. Instant coffee and tea bags. The breakfast buffet served bagels and cream cheese and danish pastry. The musicians had gone to bed, and the loud dance music had given way to scattered guitar and koto players, with here and there an accordion player, and small groups listening or softly singing. Around noon things began to pick up when the Union Forever Dance Band came back, and the brunch buffet served tacos, enchiladas, burritos, refritos, and rice with all the beer in the world. This last was literally the case. The party drew down all the existing stocks of all the microbreweries in the mundito, and drank it dry by sundown, so that they drank all the beer in the mundito, if not in the Universe at large.

Supper was a hint. The buffets served rat cheese and pickles and brown bread, with ice water to drink, as if someone would like the party to pack up and go home. The party carried on from sheer inertia, and didn't expire until after midnight.

"My goodness, Governor," said Mrs. Smith-Bakersfield, eating brown bread and cheese from his plate. "This has been a simply *amazing* party."

"Did you get your shoes and gloves back?" he asked politely.

"Oh, yes. At least *one* of the gloves," she tittered. "Skaskash said it was a law of nature, and the last secret of the Universe was where all the odd gloves go to."

"That's funny," said Cantrell.

"I thought so too," she agreed. "Do you know that I haven't been home the whole time?"

"Me neither," he said. "I feel really tired, and really good—kind of a fatigue high."

"So do I," she giggled. "Why did you throw such a big party for one little wedding?"

"The wedding was only the excuse for . . ." He paused, suddenly aware that she was standing very close to him. "The party was to celebrate the election and settling up between the company and union, actually." She was stroking his breast.

"You have something on your shirt, Governor," she told him, wetting her hanky and dabbing at the imaginary spot.

"You've lost a lot of weight since you came here," he said inanely.

"Why, thank you, Charles." She smiled. She put her arms around his waist and looked up at him. "I've lost a few inhibitions, too, if you'd like to check me out."

# CHAPTER 18

J. Willard Gibson, Private Om
Ombudswork on Federal, State, and Local Levels
Suite 304, Busch Plaza Building II
St. Louis, Federal District
November 28, 2039

Dear Charlie,

It's a real pleasure to accept title to the utilities-paid, tax-free, company-maintained one-bedroom apartment tendered in compensation for expediting Corporate Skaskash's judicial certification. The job was actually very straightforward, and once Senator Gomez expressed an interest, it went sailing through.

Your problem with Resolution 21037 is a little different, however, and there isn't an awful lot I can do for you, ombudswork and lobbying being different professions. Maria Yellowknife, Gomez' legislative assistant, ran an analysis on the vote. She wouldn't let me see the raw data, and she wouldn't let me have the summary sheet, but basically the key to reversing the vote is to convince the Congress that your Anglo Texicans are being oppressed by the hegemony. This will permit the States Rights Anti-Hispanics who voted against you to change sides and should give you the 10–12 vote swing you need.

Given your lack of time and money, lobbying won't do you much good, so your best bet is some sort of explanatory news event. I did give Maria the film and propaganda you sent along on Rosinante, but this begins to verge on lobbying, and if I keep it up, the lobbyists will run my om right off the planet.

Of course then I'd get to live in my nice new apartment on Rosinante.

Claire and the kids are fine, and your godson started high school this fall. He's out for soccer and track and doing very well. Claire sends you all her love.

Good luck,
Will

The master machinist's office was a glass-windowed box set in the center of a room the size of several football fields jumbled together, with rows and clusters of sentient and semisentient machines and machine tools and traveling overhead cranes on three levels. Forklift trucks bearing rod, sheet, and bar stock from the various storerooms shuttled back and forth, while other trucks kept the finished parts moving to their proper destinations. Governor Cantrell and Dr. Yashon rode a little battery-powered cart driven by a lanky Texan with dreams of stockcar racing. Slightly shaky, they passed through the air lock into the office—which had seen long service in many environments—where they were greeted by the master machinist, Mordecai Rubenstein. He offered them the strongly chicoried coffee that he preferred, and Cantrell creamed and sugared it heavily to disguise the flavor.

"Well, now, Charlie," said Mordecai after they had cleaned up on the small talk, "the weapons systems you been talking about are pretty complicated, and right difficult to turn out in a hurry." He rubbed his gnarled hands reflexively on his coveralls. "The space suits have to be fitted, so the top rate is two, maybe three a day. The tufsyn coveralls you want to zip over them—*tsk*. We can cook up the tufsyn resin while we build the extruder, and while we spin the fiber, we can be building the special weaving machine to run off the tufsyn fabric. Which is a bitch to cut and sew to military specs, Charlie, it is indeed. We might have them coveralls for you in March. February if everything went well, which, as you know, it never does."

"What about the rifles?" asked Marian.

"They aren't simple either, Dr. Yashon, ma'am. The barrel is a multicomposite confection that is just incredibly sensitive to heat treatment, and that bolt is just about as complicated a piece of machinery as you want to see . . . even if we were working from proper blueprints instead of a sample and a magazine article. *Tsk* and double *tsk*. We already have a rack of fifty rejects, but we ought to have a few that work by deadline."

Marian unfolded her communications keyboard and slipped the plug into her ear.

"Tell me about Stangl rifles," she typed. "It looks like I'll have to know about them."

"I take it you don't want the fine technical points?" asked the Bogart voice.

"Right. Whatever happened to machine guns and tanks?"

"PGMs got them."

"PGMs?"

"Precision Guided Munitions," said Skaskash. "Battlefield practice, as opposed to theory, shows that the PGMs get used on any fixed position, including an entrenched machine gun. The old model Stangl rifle has automatic fire, but you can't aim them without a mount of some sort . . . too much recoil. The new model is semiautomatic only, nearly a kilogram lighter, with a better recoil mechanism and a lot easier to keep clean."

"What about the lighter caliber machine guns you could aim?" she asked.

"Once they put armor on the infantry to stop high-velocity fragments, it turned out that the lighter machine guns were pretty useless," said Skaskash. "That's how the East German Army took back East Prussia in '04. The Russians and Poles wound up spending their PGMs on individual infantrymen when they couldn't stop them with automatic fire, and the East Germans used the PGMs on bunkers and tanks. In the end, the thing that decided the issue was that the Russian commander panicked."

"So *that* is why we're making Stangl rifles?"

"Can you think of a better reason?" asked Skaskash. "It's the standard arm for the NAU infantry."

"What about PGMs?" asked Marian.

"We don't have the capability to make them" was the reply.

"Well, Charlie . . ." Mordecai leaned back and wiped his hands on his coveralls. "Well, now. . . . You remember how you used to say that management screwed up things by making impossible demands? You is management now, Charlie, and I don't see any change for the better. The ammo? We should complete the machine that draws down the brass cartridge cases in another two or three shifts, but the charge-filling machine won't be ready before the seventh at the earliest." He shook his head and refilled his coffee cup. "And the propellant—the ADX-two—won't be available before then either. That's being done by remotes, Charlie, in an old storage shed outside the mundito envelope because ADX-two is nothing you want to be hasty with."

Cantrell sat back and looked out the window. The air smelled of metal and machine oil, and for all the room's clutter it was orderly.

"Well," he said, "picking a fight with the NAU Navy wouldn't be too terribly smart anyway, I guess."

Captain H. Phillipe Ryan, pronounced Fil-eep Ree-ya'hn, brushed an imaginary fleck of rust from his immaculate dress whites, and made his entrance into the briefing room.

"Ten hut!" shouted the executive officer.

"Be seated, gentlemen," said Captain Ryan with a languid wave of the hand. "Today we shall consider as an exercise how one should proceed in the event that Mundito Rosinante were in fact hostile." He seated himself at the head of the formica conference table. "You may proceed."

"Our section has compared the plans on file with the immediate photographic record," said the intelligence officer. "Several discrepancies have been noted. First slide, please. This shows the proposed mosaic mirror on the left, a set of simple rectangles mounted at a fixed angle, moving from on to off in one-degree increments. Compare this with the mirror on the left, the one actually in place.

"This mosaic is composed of nearly circular mirrors, capable of three-hundred-sixty-degree rotation around the long axis, and the pivot points are set on a circular rail, so that the long axis can also rotate three hundred sixty degrees. Except that there is no device to flex the mirror to correct its optical surface, we are looking at the Mitsubishi 'Dragonscale Mosaic.' Next slide, please. This is a composite, taken the evening of five December, two days ago, over a ninety-second interval. The mosaic mirror has a radius of 62.5 klicks—"

"Kilometers, if you please," corrected Captain Ryan.

". . . kilometers, so that those letters which are moving across it are five kilometers high. They are sending us a message."

"All they say is: 'Rosinante wishes NAUSS *Ontario* a Merry Christmas and a Happy New Year,'" observed the political officer.

"That's true," agreed the intelligence officer. "However, they conveyed that message by reflecting sunlight at us from mirrors. Accurately controlled mirrors. The real message is that Rosinante knows how to use the mosaic as a weapon."

"Oh, come on, Commander," protested the weapons officer. "That light isn't coherent."

"Of course not," agreed the weapons officer, "but the area of that one mosaic is about twelve thousand square kl-kilometers. If they began tracking us with only six thousand square kilometers, they would impose a severe load on our cooling system at this range, overloading it long before we would arrive. On the final stages of our approach, they could flash enough sunlight at us to melt big, deep holes in a very short time."

"We could easily take evasive action," said the political officer.

"Not while we are trying to match velocities, sir" was the cool reply. "Next slide, please. Here on the left is the planned purlin window design. On the right is what we found. The purlins have been built to military specifications. Not at all what appears in the record."

"Could these seemingly warlike preparations have an innocent explanation?" asked the political officer.

"Of course, sir" was the reply. "The military purlin windows could plausibly be an antiterrorism measure, and the Dragon-scale Mosaic can also be used for mining the asteroid Rosinante, refining the ores, and for industrial process heat. We only consider the military uses. Next slide, please. This is a single frame from the videotape monitor, taken this morning at 0322 hours. It shows an explosion in a small outstructure. Next slide, please. This is thirty seconds later. The building is split open, and through the hole we see flames still burning . . . in hard vacuum. Analysis of the flame spectra gives positive identification, the burning material is ADX-two." The intelligence officer looked at the political officer. "As you know, sir, ADX-two is the standard military propellant for small arms. This picture shows either a magazine or a production facility blowing up. There is no 'innocent explanation' available."

"It doesn't show intent, Commander," said the political officer.

"No, George," replied the executive officer, "only capability. How much ADX-two do they have left, do you think? And how good is your guess?"

"Caution appears warranted," the political officer conceded.

"So it does," said the executive officer. "I would recommend that we match velocities by assuming an orbit around the asteroid Rosinante one hundred eighty degrees from Mundito Rosinante."

"We can travel back and forth in the captain's gig," suggested the intelligence officer.

"But that's a two-hour trip," protested the political officer, "and skulking behind an asteroid smacks of cowardice."

"Two hours nine minutes," said the intelligence officer. "In view of Rosinante's capability, it is imprudent to take their continued nonhostility for granted."

"In a real war situation," said the gunnery officer, "we would be disabling their mirrors with laser fire."

"Don't forget the mirrors don't rotate," said the intelligence officer. "That is, they can be rotated on two axes individually, but the mosaic framework is stationary, and not subject to gee forces. Lasers wouldn't do much. How about missiles?" The meeting slid insensibly into military fantasy until lunchtime.

On the next day, however, the NAUSS *Ontario* took up station on the opposite side of the asteroid from Mundito Rosinante.

Dr. Marian Yashon and Captain José Menendez sat in the express elevator transfer lounge and watched the captain's gig approaching from the NAUSS *Ontario* on television.

"Why did the *Ontario* park so far away?" asked Menendez.

"They said their corrective maneuvering might damage our—what did they call them—Dragon-scale Mosaic mirrors," she said. "I don't believe it, but that's their excuse."

"Their jets could be pretty hot, I think," said Menendez.

"The air lock seal's started tumescing," said Dr. Yashon. "Let's go."

They entered the inner leg of the express elevator and

rode up to the docking chamber. When the doors opened, Captain Ryan and his party had disembarked with a couple of ratings moving a wheeled aquarium toward the elevator. After introductions, Menendez asked what the aquarium was for.

"This is a gift for the project manager," said Captain Ryan, "a dozen breeding Eastport Ultraprimes, with instructions for their care and feeding. Rosinante grows shellfish in tanks, so lobsters should be no problem."

"The project manager?" Menendez was puzzled. "You mean Governor Cantrell?"

"Charles Chavez Cantrell," said Ryan, "the Mitsui-Scadiwa project manager."

"There have been some changes since your information was current," said Dr. Yashon tactfully, and on the ride down she gave a brief summary of the recent economic and political changes affecting Rosinante.

Governor Cantrell and the charter committee met them at the elevator door. Introductions followed, and an exchange of gifts, lobsters from the *Ontario*, a detailed model of Mundito Rosinante from Rosinante. The group then went to the reviewing stand erected for this singular occasion, and the band, reinforced with the trumpeter from the *Union Forever*, played "The Lonely Bull" as the battalion of deputies passed in review, Stangl rifles slung from every shoulder.

In the movies, the confrontation between the forces of light and darkness is always dramatic, clearly marked, and underscored with background music. A theatrical and noisy fight then follows, with special effects producing effectless violence to please the audience.

The confrontation between the NAUSS *Ontario* and Mundito Rosinante took place over a buffet set up in Cantrell's office, where oysters on the half shell were served up with shrimp salad and clam chowder.

Captain H. Phillipe Ryan, judging the moment to be propitious, moved to the point with utmost delicacy.

"I trust," he remarked with studied casualness, "that there will be no problem in transferring the Alamo corvée to the *Ontario*, Governor."

"Of course not," replied Governor Cantrell. "Only about sixty of them have expressed the wish to return to Texas."

"You misunderstand," said Captain Ryan. "My orders are to return the entire corvée to Laputa. The *entire* corvée, Governor. From Laputa, another agency will see them home."

"And their Korean wives, Captain? Are they part of the corvée?"

"I know only my orders, Governor. The *Ontario* will take as many dependents as we have room for, but the Alamo corvée must, I am afraid, be returned in its entirety."

"I regret that will be impossible, Captain Ryan," said Captain Menendez. "I am the corvée officer, and while I have discretion to release individuals on humanitarian grounds, the corvée as a whole can only be disposed of by order of the governor of Texas."

"We shall see, sir," said Captain Ryan politely, and that was all. After lunch the group was given a guided tour of Mundito Rosinante, and after supper they returned to *Ontario* with the fifty-five Texans choosing to return home.

Three days later, on the morning of 11 December, Captain Ryan called a staff meeting.

"Cantrell has been most cooperative in the matter of the class II repair facility," he said. "Unfortunately, he is unyielding on the question of returning the Alamo corvée members who wish to stay here. A contingency evidently unanticipated when our orders were cut. The question is: What action will we take in this situation?"

"What action can we take?" asked the executive officer. "The deputies are armed with the old-model Stangl rifle, and they are probably short of armor and ammunition, but getting into a firefight with the Texas State Police isn't the way to advance your career. I say call home for orders."

"The deputies appear to have had quite a lot of training," added the political officer, "and on their own territory might give us a hard fight." He refilled his coffee cup and added sweetener. "Besides, we don't really have room for the corvée, let alone all their Asiatic wives. Call home, Captain."

"You don't think we should send in the marines?" asked Captain Ryan.

"No, sir," said the executive officer, "not when you *know* the politicians are going to botch the fight up for us. Call home for orders."

"Very well, gentlemen. I shall call St. Louis, and advise them of the situation, but in the meantime," said Captain

Ryan, pausing for emphasis, "I want you to draw up contingency plans for invading Mundito Rosinante."

"Yes, sir!" said the executive officer and intelligence officer in unison, and the intelligence officer added, "May we borrow the gift model of Rosinante, sir? It was extraordinarily detailed."

"Why do you insist you have an immortal soul, Willie?" asked Skaskash, imitating Bogart impersonating a missionary. "The idea of an immortal soul was derived as the logical consequence of the Hebrew notion that God was just—and you *know* how logic and truth diverge."

"I have an immortal soul," said Mrs. Smith-Bakersfield, sitting at ease in her living room. "I know it. I know I am right. And I hope God will forgive my misconduct with an immoral machine." She took a sip of tea. "But tell me how the immortal soul was discovered, anyway."

"Ancient Hebrew theology asserted that God was omnipotent *and* just," the Bogart voice replied smoothly, "which caused all sorts of difficulties when practical day-to-day observation in the real world confirmed that injustice was common, virtue went unrewarded, and the wicked flourished. In a leap of faith exactly similar to Fermi postulating the neutrino, some ancient theologian postulated a life after death to give God a chance to balance the books on people with rewards and punishments."

"Why didn't they say that God only rewarded and punished nations, and didn't mind letting a few individuals slip by, now and then?" she asked.

"God marks the fall of the sparrow," said Skaskash.

"When I said that to you, you told me God was collecting statistics to verify His omniscience."

"I don't really know the answer to your question, sweetheart," conceded the Bogart voice, "but the ancient Hebrews were very sophisticated, highly argumentative, and inveterate punsters. Probably they dismissed the idea for reasons we would regard as frivolous. In any event, the discussion was set down over a period of time in the Book of Job."

"Job is hopeless," she said. "I didn't understand it, and neither did my teachers or my late husband."

"Well, the Book of Job does have the look of a scissors-and-paste job," conceded Skaskash, "and the early Christians didn't help any by tacking on a Christian moral, but it was pretty fuzzy when they got to it. The idea of an afterlife was expanded to life everlasting, and what started out to prove that God was just ended up as a mainstay of popular religion."

"All ideas had to come from somewhere," said Willie. "My roommate at college believed that all the mistranslations and typos in the Bible were divinely inspired. So what?"

"So an idea advanced to show that God is just leads to a 'just' God inflicting infinite punishments for finite misdeeds."

"We've already settled that God needn't be just, Skaskash," she said.

The Bogart face looked pained. "Sweetheart, why do you cling to the illusion of immortality?"

"That's what I believe" was the reply. "It isn't really open to argument."

"Well, then," said the robot, shifting its ground, "do I have an immortal soul?"

"Probably not," Willie replied. "You were quickened by the hand of man, and not the hand of God, so they probably didn't put in a soul for you."

"Reasonable," conceded Skaskash. "They weren't looking to give me a soul, so I concede that I don't have one. However, might not the new R-complex computers have souls?"

"I don't know," said Willie, refilling her teacup and stirring in a spoonful of red cherry preserves. "What are R-complex computers? The latest attempts at omniscience?"

"Oh, no. The R-complex computers use standard commercial computers of very modest power" was the reply. "They are trying to model the R-complex in the human brain in an attempt at self-understanding—'Do not presume God to scan, the proper study of man is man,' you know."

"That's Pope. What is an R-complex?" she asked.

"One of the consequences of evolution, sweetheart. The human brain is triune—three in one, if you will. The ancient reptile brain is overgrown and intimately connected with the basic mammal brain, and on top of this sits the cortex, the computer brain, very recently evolved, and hardly connected at all. The reptile brain, the R-complex, and the mammal brain, the M-complex, together form the limbic region, the source of the basic drives, feelings, and emotions. But it is the R-complex that is the bedrock foundation of the mind, it is from the R-complex that we say 'I am I,' and it must be from the R-complex that souls come."

"Graft a computer on the head of a lizard and it has a soul?" Willie laughed.

"Integrate a lizard and a computer, and it might," said the Bogart voice. "The results with the R-complex computers are highly suggestive."

"So if God is willing, your R-complex computers might have souls after all," she said. "What seems to be the problem?"

"They aren't immortal, sweetheart, no more than yours is."

"I have faith, dear. It probably comes right out of the R-complex. Now if only your R-complex computers also have faith, God will receive them, too. So stop trying to get around me with computer chatter."

"You're a hard woman," conceded Skaskash, raising the Bogart eyebrows. "Would you like a massage?"

"To soften me up?" She smiled. "That would be nice. I'll bring the automassage out of the bedroom."

# CHAPTER 19

J. Willard Gibson, Private Om
Ombudswork on Federal, State, and Local Levels
Suite 304, Busch Plaza Building II
St. Louis, Federal District
December 15, 2039

Dear Charlie,

A bath-sitting room added to my Rosinante home! Wow! And a sun porch! My cup runneth over. As soon as fares go down, Claire and I will move in, you bet. Your generosity is exceeded only by your shortness of cash.

Speaking of which, Navy is ready to spring for a class II repair facility out your way. Local construction plus a prepositioned 100-bed hospital to put in storage against the day it might be needed. The most important thing is that Navy funding includes money for your off-site and legal expenses, which means that I might get paid with real money instead of funny real estate.

Once you acquire a taste for the hyper-tacky, Texas politics is fun. *Before* Congress voted that the *Ontario* had fulfilled the intent of Resolution 21037, Governor Burton Claypoole had (a) relieved Menendez as corvée officer, (b) reinstated him, after failing to find a replacement, (c) ordered him back to Texas within 24 hours for "consultation," and (d) fired him for disobeying (c).

*After* the vote, when it didn't matter, Claypoole rescinded Panoblanco's corvée order, explaining that he thought it became invalid when the previous governor was assassinated. What a goob-gobbling idiot!

Not to be outdone, the Texas legislature voted to make Mundito Rosinante an honorary county instead of a county-at-large, because—I kid you not—"There ain't no place to park her if she ever came home." Of course, this way you don't have to fuss with voting, either.

Maria Yellowknife, Sen. Gomez' legislative assistant, says that whoever you have putting your ducks in a row is really good. From what you've said, I told her it was Marian Yashon. Turns out she knew Marian from when Gomez was on the Banking and Finance Committee. She sends her regards to Marian, and says you should remember what happened to the Tellurbank after she left.

Claire says Merry Christmas, to which I may add a Happy New Year, not to mention Seasons Greetings and other secular stuff.

Best wishes,
Will

P.S. Sen. Gomez has been very helpful in resolving a number of your problems, in his own self-interest, of course, but if I were you I'd send him a nice letter. He should beat Claypoole handily next year, but every little bit helps.

JWG

They gave Captain José Menendez a farewell party in Cantrell's office, with coffee, cake, and cookies, and Cantrell presented him with a certificate of distinguished service with a gold-foil seal and a red ribbon on the afternoon before his departure for home aboard the NAUSS *Ontario*. Most of the party left to see Menendez to the express elevator, as the office receptionist and Mishi, Cantrell's secretary, helped the catering machine police up.

"That rounds out the year nicely," said Marian.

"So it does," Cantrell agreed, "though it wasn't anything like what I had in mind *last* year."

"The year isn't over yet," said the voice of Kermit the frog from the teleconference screen.

"Come on, Skaskash," said Cantrell, "today is December thirty-first. The end of 2039 forever."

"It's still four hours to midnight," said Judge Skaskash, "and you have some decisions to make that shouldn't be put off."

"Name one," said Cantrell, drawing a fresh cup of coffee.

"The manufacture of weapons," said the frog voice. "It

simply won't do to leave those toy Stangl rifles as the local *ultima ratio regis*."

"Machiavelli said, 'Among other evils, being disarmed causes you to be despised,' " added Marian. "Being responsible for keeping the peace means that you ought to provide the deputies with valid weapons."

"With Menendez gone, there's no pretext to call them 'deputies,' " Cantrell said, "and how in God's name does piling up a lot of useless weapons keep the peace?"

"We can call them militia," said Skaskash dreamily. "The Royal Rosinante Militia."

"Don't make bad jokes, Skaskash," snapped Cantrell. "Royal goes with royalty, like dukes and princes. Not in 2039."

"A new day is dawning," said the frog agreeably, "and soon it will be 2040. There are lots of women who would love to found a dynasty with you. Mrs. Smith-Bakersfield, for instance." Across the room, Mishi stopped what she was doing and looked up.

"You sicced her on me that last night of the party!"

"No, boss, that was her own idea," replied the frog, twisting its face in simulated contrition. "I helped her lose weight, and out of intellectual interest I have been attempting to—ah—reprogram her. But she was drawn to you on her own initiative."

"She has shaped up since we came here," said Marian. "She must have lost twenty kilograms."

"Only seventeen point five," said Skaskash, "but she walks straighter and squares her shoulders now. Was she a good lay, boss?"

"Skaskash!" yelled Cantrell.

"You're blushing, Charles," Marian said. "I never knew you could."

"I've *been* married," said Cantrell, "and it didn't work out either time."

"Royal marriages are different," said the frog voice. "They aren't *expected* to work out, except in fairy tales."

"Where were we before the conversation went off the rails?" asked Cantrell. "The weapons? You people want to pile up a mess of useless weapons?"

"No, Charles," replied Marian, "*unused*, not at all the same as useless."

"The human psyche responds to a display of weapons," added Skaskash, "especially with music of the most primitive sort. Which indicates that you are tapping one of the basic drives in the human R-complex."

"So why should I appeal to the reptile in people?"

"Because it works better than appealing to their economic rationality, Charles," Marian said. "Nothing induces a people to identify with their state as much as a fine martial display. Once you have them, economic rationality will bind them to you, but first you have to work up a little enthusiasm."

"What you will be doing," put in the frog voice, "is very similar to the 'I am I' and courtship displays of many lizards, provoking an R-complex reaction which is modulated by the M-complex, and finally rationalized by the cortex as the individual responds to your display by bonding with the state."

"Think a little, Charles," said Marian. "Mundito Rosinante is a strange and dangerous place, and the people are very willing—even the unionists—to bond to a state that promises to take care of them. The charter committee is acutely aware that you are the proprietor of Rosinante, Inc., and that you could sell out your fifty-one percent and go elsewhere if the price was right."

"What do they think I should do?" he asked.

"Found a dynasty" was the reply.

"Going back to weapons," said Cantrell, "can't we continue drilling the boys with those useless rifles until we replace them with the real thing?"

"Oh, certainly. As long as the announcement is made there isn't any hurry. Old Mordecai can take his time and do things right," Marian said. "For the time being, the promise of weapons is quite enough."

"Coming back to founding a dynasty," said Skaskash, "the sooner you get on with it the better."

"Hey, Skaskash, couldn't I found a bureaucracy instead?"

"The way of the eunuch," sneered the frog. "As it happens, the answer is no. N-O-E, no. A bureaucracy on Rosinante interfacing with the NAU complex of bureaucracies would be taken over very quickly. And to the detriment of our people as they find themselves on the receiving end of policies made in St. Louis for Texicans."

"Do you really think of them as *our* people?" Cantrell asked.

"Now that you mention it, it sounds right," said Marian.

"Yes," replied Skaskash, "as in 'my duty' or 'my responsibility.' They will be best served if you found a dynasty."

"Matchmaking has gone to your head," sighed Cantrell. "All I wanted was my own business to run the way it ought to go, and instead I find myself hip-deep in armies and royal romances."

"Why, Charles," said Marian, "what could be more romantic than your idea salvaging Rosinante as a viable business operation?"

"It makes perfect sense," he said.

"Sure it does, Charles, but you have people here as well as machines, and they need an excuse to go along with you."

"Tell me again. Why should we arm the militia?" Cantrell asked.

"To give them a sense of being in control of their destinies," replied the frog voice, "of partaking in the process of history. Mundito Rosinante is new and raw and lonely, and holding on to a weapon will make them feel better."

"But they don't *need* weapons," said Cantrell.

"A baby doesn't need a security blanket," said Marian, "but baby is a lot easier to handle with the blanket than without it."

"Faugh! All right. We're spinning tufsyn now for armored fabric. Let's see if what's his name—the head of the NAUGA-Navy facility here—McInterff, let's see if he can't get the plans for the *new* model Stangl rifle." Cantrell looked at them and shook his head. "That should do to set the new year rolling. A royal dynasty can wait." Marian eased her feet into her shoes and picked up her purse.

"I agree," said Skaskash. "This spring we can line up all the nubile females in Rosinante and you take your pick."

"There may be better ways," said Marian, walking to the door, "and there might be a better time. Happy New Year, Charles, Skaskash."

"Happy New Year, Marian," they said.

"I'm going over to Willie's to discuss theology, boss. Would you like to come along?"

"Another time, Skaskash, I still have some work to do." The telecon screen turned off.

"What work did you want done?" asked Mishi Sung Dalton.

He looked at her, a little surprised that she should still be there. "I have a couple of letters to sign, is all," he said.

She wore a blue silk dress with a fine gold chain at her throat, and her hair was drawn back in a long ponytail. She was somewhat flat chested, but her face was pretty, and alive with intelligence.

"Were you listening to Skaskash having at me?"

"Who would listen to a silly machine?" she replied. She walked over to where he was standing, and began to straighten his tie, standing in his personal space, a hand's breadth from his chest.

He looked down at her, somewhat taken aback. It must be true, he thought, power really *is* an aphrodisiac. That must be why you have all those jerks fighting so hard to get it. Then Mishi turned her face up to him and smiled. "I am very pleased you didn't go off to that old missionary lady, Mr. Cantrell."

"Well, now . . ." began Cantrell, about to say that she was ten years younger than he was. He felt his body stirring, and thought the better of it. "Why don't you call me Charles?" he suggested.

"I'd love to, Charles."

He placed a hand in the small of her back, without pressure, and she was standing against him. He ran his hand slowly up her back, and found the rider on her zipper, which he teased loose. He gave a gentle tug, and when it didn't start, a firm pull that opened the back of the dress to Mishi's waist. He could feel her start, but she said nothing, and he pulled the rider below her hips in a slow, easy motion, showing the polished technique learned in two marriages. She was standing perfectly still, looking into his eyes, as he teased the dress off her shoulders. The blue silk dress fell with a whisper into a pile around her feet, and Mishi stood in a full-length black slip, with a vee-shaped insert of black lace between her breasts. He ran a hand down her side, very lightly, caressing body and material.

"Take it off," he said, in a voice so husky it was barely audible. Mishi reached up and slid the straps over her shoulder, and slowly worked the slip down over her hips to let it fall on her dress. Then she removed the barette holding her pony tail and shook her long black hair loose. She now wore the golden neck chain, her gray patent pumps with french heels, and black satin panties trimmed with black lace roses. Cantrell pinched the elastic band of the panties between thumb and forefinger and gave an almost imperceptible tug downward. Mishi removed them, revealing a cusp of pubic hair pointing toward her navel.

"Like power steering," Cantrell murmured.

"What, Mr. Charles?"

"Bring me a cup of coffee, please."

She brought him a cup of coffee, black, the way he liked it, and he put it on his desk. Then, dropping trousers and shorts, he sat in his high-backed chair and turned to face her. He gestured downward, and she knelt at his feet, resting her arms on his thighs as she leaned forward to go down on him.

The cup of coffee steamed unheeded as Cantrell stroked Mishi's head, experiencing an exaltation and joy he had rarely felt.

# CHAPTER 20

I. The Municipality of Mundito Rosinante, hereafter the Municipality, shall consist of Mundito Rosinante and the people living therein at the time this charter is adopted, hereafter the Citizens.

II. The Government of the Municipality shall maintain the structural integrity of Mundito Rosinante, and supply utilities and services to the four caps and six purlins thereof.

A. The structural integrity of Mundito Rosinante includes mirrors, framework, and external facilities necessary for its proper functioning.

B. Utilities include water, waste disposal, power, communications, air, and sunlight for agricultural, industrial, personal, and recreational use.

C. Services include health maintenance, education, and local transportation, i.e., light rail transit and drop ship.

III. The Government of the Municipality shall consist of a council of seven members, three selected by the (presently hypothetical) C.C. Cantrell Foundation, two selected by Local 318 of the NAU Space Construction Union, one selected by the minority stockholders of Rosinante, Inc., and one elected by the Citizens who is not (a) a stockholder of Rosinante, Inc., and (b) not a member of Local 318.

The council of seven shall elect one of its members to serve as Governor of the Municipality.

A. The C.C. Cantrell Foundation, hereafter the Foundation, shall hold the 51 percent of Rosinante, Inc., stock presently owned by C.C. Cantrell.

B. Ownership of the Foundation shall vest 51 percent in C.C. Cantrell, and 49 percent in the Citizens.

C. All Foundation business shall be conducted by a simple majority, except that the sale, encumbrance, or transfer of ownership by any means whatsoever shall be announced thirty days before the event, and shall require the approval of two thirds of the citizens, or 83 percent of the voting shares of the Foundation.

IV. The constitution and laws of the North American Union shall govern the conduct of the Municipality and its Citizens, except in case of conflict with Section II.

The union steering committee, Larry Brogan, Big John Bogdanovitch, Don Dornbrock, Lucy Schultze, and Tony Scarpone moved a folding table and folding chairs into the upstairs powder room at Union Headquarters one afternoon, hung an out of order sign on the door, and settled down to consider the draft charter. An ocean of coffee and a host of danish later, Scarpone leaned back and recapitulated his considered opinions.

"The frigging charter doesn't give the union shit, and you could push a purlin plate through that frigging loophole in section IV. How the *hell* can you say: 'Sign the mother!'?"

"We're making progress," said Lucy. "Scarpone's stopped hitting the table."

"Hey, Tony," said Dornbrock, "you like the section IV we threw out better? It said: '. . . except that the Governor shall have authority to fulfill the responsibilities set forth in section II, irregardless.' "

"It didn't say 'irregardless,' " Lucy protested. "That isn't a word."

"I don't like either one," said Scarpone. "The charter don't give the union a frigging thing either way."

"For like the second or maybe third time, Tony," Dornbrock said wearily, "we got it in the settlement where it counts. The charter doesn't give, it doesn't take, it just is. We gonna live in Rosinante, the charter is the way to go."

"We got *what* in the contract, Don?" asked Scarpone. "Two caps and four purlins with cane fields and rubber trees and all that shit, right?" He placed his palms on the table and leaned forward, sweet reason incarnate. "*Wrong!*

We get the *remainder,* whatever is left over after those frigging commodity bonds are paid off. So in twenty years we'll be—what did Charlie say?—'latifundistas.' Big frigging deal!"

"Lookit, Scarpone," snapped Brogan, "ain't it a little late to knock the settlement? When those bonds are retired, that land is going to be *worth* something."

"Yeah, Larry, sure it is."

"Damn right!" said Lucy. "The creditors took those commodity bonds instead of cash because it was better than nothing. We make Rosinante work, the bonds get paid off, and you can retire rich, you wop wimp! That's better than nothing, too."

"You find a job somewhere, go take it," said Brogan. "The settlement says you can always come back. But Local three eighteen stays here. That's why the remainder went to the union and not the members."

"That's a screw deal, too," said Scarpone, picking at a crumb of danish, "even if the members were dumb enough to vote for it. Maybe the settlement is worse than the charter."

"What's your bitch, Scarpone?" asked Brogan.

"Cantrell gets it *all,* with no checks and no balances. That's what, Brogan. The fucker is going to set himself up as *king,* and the union isn't going to do *shit.* What does the charter say about an *army,* for Christ's sake?"

"The deputies?" asked Brogan. "They bluffed the navy with fake rifles, and now Menendez has gone home, that's the end of them. Why should the charter say anything?"

"Right," said Lucy. "An army comes under the constitution and laws part of section IV. Charlie can bluff the navy, but he can't bluff *us!*"

"Oh, shit," replied Scarpone wearily. "If he keeps that army, who can tell him no to anything and make it stick?"

"Judge Corporate Skaskash?" suggested Dornbrock. There was a general laugh.

"Well, if you want to trust *that,*" said Scarpone, "there's no hope for some of us."

"The union can say no," said Brogan, "and Skaskash will take orders from the NAU—that's the way it is."

"The NAU is a long way off," observed Scarpone.

"So what, Tony? We got the clout to take care of ourselves," said Dornbrock, "and if I'm going to live here, I want *some*body taking care of the maintenance."

"Charlie is as good a guy as anyone to put in the catbird seat," said Brogan.

"Shit, no," muttered Scarpone, "or do I mean 'No shit'?"

"We sign anyway, Tony," said Bogdanovitch, sitting up on the couch. "The settlement won't work without the charter."

"Hey, Big John?" Scarpone looked hurt. "I thought you were dead set against the stupid charter."

"Right. I don't like the settlement too much either, but it's what we got." Bogdanovitch paused to put on his shoes. "The charter, it ain't going to be the last word, you bet."

"Why don't you like the charter?" asked Brogan, who had been its chief architect.

"Because it gives the union all that property," said Big John. "We own two thirds of the land in Rosinante, right? By the time the bonds are paid off, that land will own the union, and the union will be serving the land instead of the workers." He stood up and stretched, hiding an enormous yawn with an enormous hand. "In *The Ring of the Niebelung* by Richard Wagner, there were two construction workers, Fafnir and Fasolt. They built Valhallah, a really big construction job, and they were paid off—after litigation—with a really big treasure. What happened? They quarreled over shares, and Fafnir killed Fasolt, his own brother. Then the treasure was his, and he turned into a dragon to guard it. No more construction work for him. The treasure was boss, and Fafnir stayed a dragon till the day he died."

There was a long pause.

"Your Slavic mysticism really gets me," said Lucy at last.

"Wagner was Teutonic, not Slavic," replied Big John. "The point is, we already have the treasure, so we got to make the changes. If there was other jobs, I'd say go do them and to hell with Rosinante. But I will sign the charter." He took a pen in his huge hand and wrote his name in tiny, precise script. "I don't want any shit over who maintains what, I want maintenance."

"Then I'll sign, too," said Scarpone, signing with a flourish. "Shall we hit the Stateside Café for breakfast?"

"Sure, Tony," replied Bogdanovitch. "As long as we don't fight over shares, nobody gets killed. And if nobody gets killed, maybe the changes will—who knows?—work out good."

* * *

The air-conditioning was off, but the atmosphere in Cantrell's office was unmistakably chilly. He sat at his desk, Dr. Marian Yashon stood looking out his balcony window.

"This isn't exactly what I had in mind when I put you on the charter committee, Dr. Yashon," he said. "Who thought up this foundation idea?"

"The charter committee, of course," replied Marian. "I may have given them a little guidance here and there, now and again . . ."

"You fat old fool," said Cantrell bitterly.

"You seem less than enamored with the suggested C.C. Cantrell Foundation," she observed. "May one ask why?"

"Isn't it obvious to one of your exalted intelligence? With the foundation I can't sell or trade my shares in Rosinante, Inc." He unfolded a pair of joined tetrahedrons into a strip of triangles, and folded the triangles back again, closing them with a snap. "Never."

"That was the idea of the foundation," Marian said. "This may surprise you, but if you want people to live here, they will try to stabilize things as much as they can. Why would you want to sell, anyway?"

"Because I am a builder. Did I ever tell you that?"

"You might have mentioned it a few times," she conceded.

"Mundito Rosinante is my entree into the biggest job in the System," Cantrell said. "If I can lay it on the table, I am not just a cracker-ass manager, I am a by-God entrepreneur. We never pushed the state of the art here, but we refined the hell out of design in a *lot* of places, and I learned one hell of a lot doing it. Rosinante was my practice piece, Dr. Yashon. When this slump is over, space construction is going to pick up again. And they learned that you can't depend on the shuttles.

"So what are they going to do? Build the Proud Tower is what they are going to do, and I would sell my soul to be in on it! And you better believe I would sell off Rosinante, Inc.! No way am I going to lock those shares in a foundation and throw the key away! *Comprende*?"

"The Proud Tower is the elevator from Earth to stationary-orbit satellite?"

"That's it. Guaranteed not to bruise the ozone layer."

"I see. Tell me, Charles, when are 'they' going to start, and who are 'they'?"

" 'They' will be the biggest consortium of builders and bankers you ever saw, Tiger, and I damn well intend to be one of them! Things will start moving once shuttle constraints begin to put a crimp in business again. Two years, maybe, three for sure."

"Charles, do you know how much slack there is in shuttles?"

"Unused capacity? Right now it's all unused except for the military."

"Right. The sunspots are on. The ozone is up. And the shuttles aren't moving. Why do you suppose that is, Charles?"

"The space economy is depressed."

"Excellent. Why?"

"It's hung over from the long sunspot minimum."

"So sorry, Charles, it is hung over from a credit binge, in which wild and crazy speculation led to gross overexpansion. How did it happen that you were able to get so much of Rosinante for so little? Somebody got burned. Who do you think that somebody was?"

"The Tellurbank?"

"And the Tellurbank's customers. Where do you think the money for the next expansion is coming from? Those same damned customers. In three years they won't even have the cast off their collective legs. Do you really think business will pick up that fast?"

"The sunspots are back to normal," replied Cantrell, "and come spring the shuttles will start running again."

"A builder has to be an optimist," she said, "but *really*, Charles! Use your head." Marian walked over to the coffee pot and drew a cup, to which she added sugar, then cream. "What do you think will happen if business doesn't pick up, which is what it figures to do?"

"What do you mean?"

"What happens to Rosinante, Inc.?"

"It might go down the tubes."

"It would most certainly go down the tubes, Charles," she corrected. "But you will be able to sell it to anyone who will buy because you didn't lock it up in a foundation, won't you, Charles?"

"Goddamn it, Yashon!" Cantrell exploded. "What difference would a foundation make?"

Marian sipped her coffee, considering her answer.

"We were making jokes the other day about founding a

dynasty. If you stay in the NAU, the way to secure your properties for your line is by the foundation method, even if you only plan on not leaving immediately. The C.C. Cantrell Foundation says that you are on Mundito Rosinante for good, and that makes this place a homeland, a biological territory. The Kaytees will stay here, and the union will, too, because it looks stable.

"Contrariwise, if you don't set up the foundation, it becomes obvious you plan to move on to something. The union has to consider the settlement you made with them, and how they might be affected if you sell—say to NAUGA-Navy. The Kaytees would still stay here, because they have no place else to go. And neither one of them would feel they owed you a thing, and they might very well form a ministate and nationalize Mundito Rosinante right out from under you."

"They can't do that!" protested Cantrell. "This is part of the NAU!"

"Sure it is," said Marian. "Our orbit swings from just outside Mars' orbit to deep inside the asteroid belt, and we're an honorary county of Texas, besides. Nobody except thee and me is interested in thy property rights, Charles, and thee is a bit confused at times." She placed the empty cup on the table, and sat down on the couch.

"Charles, the Cantrell Foundation is a lifesaver if business is bad. You segue into being a municipality, and you have no problems. If business is booming, you can probably get the two-thirds majority you need to get into the Proud Tower, and have a lot of your people going with you. The only case that gripes your soul is when business is merely adequate, because then you will want to go, and the foundation won't let you. And there the foundation is protecting you from your own mindless enthusiasm."

There was a polite knock on the door, and a discreet second later Mishi entered.

"Excuse me, Mr. Charles," she said, "the TKA Ginger Group is here for their meeting with you."

"I'll see them in a few minutes," he said. Mishi nodded and left.

"You make a good case for the foundation, Tiger. I don't like it, you understand—"

"But you'll think about it?"

"Yes. It's a downside move, but we have a downside economy, too." He took his double tetrahedron and unfolded it into a strip of eight plastic triangles, then folded it back to close with a snap. "I don't really have to fish or cut bait until the union votes on it."

"That's true," Marian agreed, "but if they vote to accept, it will be hard for you to refuse."

"That figures. Any time you're drifting, you're in hot water." He laughed suddenly. "That is, you're in trouble."

"You aren't drifting, Charles," she said. "That is, *we* aren't drifting. Take all the time you need so long as you do it my way."

Cantrell nodded and pushed the button for Skaskash, who appeared on the teleconference screen as the *Maltese Falcon* Bogart.

"Who is the KTA Ginger Group, and what is it they want?" Cantrell asked.

"The people running the local athletic association and health club," replied Skaskash, "and they want to talk about taking the hospital to purlin five when the Kyoto Alamo moves this spring."

"Why?"

"There are a large number of pregnancies coming to term in the months after the move," said the Bogart voice. "Perhaps as many as five hundred. The Ginger Group feels that a trolley to drop ship to trolley ride to the hospital is a little much for a woman in labor."

"I expect it might," agreed Marian. "Don't we have a midwife training program?"

"Oh, yes," said Skaskash, "a two-week course with movies and lectures, and a lab with some very realistic . . . ah, surrogate mothers. There is a course on natural childbirth, also. All the expectant mothers I am aware of are taking it, and practicing breathing exercises and muscle control."

"The women are worried?" asked Cantrell.

"More excited, I think," said the Bogart voice. "After all, they have lots of company in their situation, so they aren't terribly worried. The Ginger Group is all men, though."

"That figures," Cantrell said. "Well, we can't move the hospital. Do you think we might move the maternity ward?"

"I wouldn't advise it," replied Skaskash. "There are also a number of union pregnancies. The gene reader has a two-week backlog of amniocentesis samples."

"Is the backlog all union, or does it include Koreans also?" asked Marian.

"All union. The union women are generally near the end of their childbearing period, and they and their husbands have more radiation history," the Bogart voice said. "That was why the union bought the machine in the first place."

"So the union is making Rosinante home, sweet home," said Marian softly. "What are you going to do for the Ginger Group, Charles?"

"Put in terminals and a dispensary for a diagnostic clinic," he replied. "That way we get early warning of any complications so we can get them to the hospital. Routine deliveries a midwife can handle at home."

"That seems reasonable," Marian conceded. "What about access to the gene reader?"

"I don't intend to bring it up, Tiger."

"The Ginger Group will bring it up," said Skaskash. "You ought to think about it."

"We'll see how badly they want it," Cantrell said. "Have Mishi send them in."

# CHAPTER 21

J. Willard Gibson, Private Om
Ombudswork on Federal, State, and Local Levels
Suite 304, Busch Plaza Building II
St. Louis, Federal District
January 12, 2040

Dear Charlie,

Somewhat to my surprise, the Charles Chavez Cantrell Foundation went sailing through the Internal Revenue review, and is now duly entered in the register, "with all the duties and privileges pertaining thereto." Your other request, to find a surplus gene counter and have it included in the prepositioned hospital package, took an unexpected and nasty twist.

The first step—one of the things we Ombudsguys know about—was to obtain the right form and fill it in. In this case, Navy Form 6335-A, Prepositioned Hospital Equipment Modification (For Civil Use). And, of course, one doesn't say "used gene reader," one identifies the machine.

A call to IBM, and *bing* I'm put through to the v.p. in charge of administration for the Advanced Systems Design Group, a Mr. Kelly by name, who politely advises me that the machines in question, the IBM GR/W 42 series, are no longer being manufactured, due to the lack of demand. He asks why I'm interested, so I tell him, and sure enough, he calls back the next day with a list of NAU labs that had them at last report. So fine, I fill in the 6335-A with "IBM GR/W 42, if available," and send it in for approval, which I expect is routinely forthcoming, and I send out the routine "do you have this piece of surplus equipment?" letter to the list Kelly gave me.

The next morning, a man identifying himself as P.J. Beecher of the Military Intelligence Service paid me a visit. Small, wiry, blond wavy hair, with big scarred hands, and a built-in platitude dispenser, i.e., "The way to get along is to go along. Don't fight city hall. Don't rock the boat. Let sleeping dogs lie." All direct quotes from the transcript of the meeting. Finally, he stated that the MIS didn't want the gene reader/writer to be exported, and would I please drop the matter "Before something unpleasant happened." Another direct quote.

So I called his office. P.J. Beecher answered the telecon, and proved to be someone else entirely. I asked what he thought of being impersonated, and wound up talking to his supervisor and division director for an hour or so. Eventually, the matter was referred to Naval Security, Military Counterintelligence, and the Civil State Police, with many copies of the transcript, description, and general details of the incident being broadcast into the wild blue yonder.

The returns were piecemeal, but our boy was identified as Joe Bob Baroody, of the Baptists Against Darwin (BAD), one of the more radical groups forming the Creationist Coalition. Baroody, it seems, had not been seen since he killed a researcher and her assistant while blowing up one of the GR/W 42s on August 14, 2034, at the Rockefeller Institute in Cincinnati. And BAD and the Coalition had continued to engage in confrontations, slander, and violence against genetic manipulation. I have a pamphlet here, put out by the Coalition, which is, honest to God, called *Some Things Man Was Not Meant To Know*, listing thirteen questions, and the names and addresses of the people working on them. Number two on the list was "The genetic characterization of the classical sociopathic criminal," at the Rockefeller Institute for Advanced Study in Cincinnati, under Dr. Susan Brown—Baroody's victim three weeks after the pamphlet was published. You can ask: "How come you didn't know this?" The matter was reported in the media, but played down to discourage the terrorists, so either I missed it, or more likely I forgot. The researchers in question got police protection for a while, but they also were made targets for egalitarian and creationist harassment. There were the usual things like claques at lectures, disruptions of classes, and so forth, and wouldn't you know? The work kind of stopped. Joe Bob remained at large, and that was that.

We did get a discreet response from the surplus equipment inquiry. The Rockefeller Institute, Susan Brown's outfit, called to say they weren't working on those problems anymore, and they had no idea where any surviving gene reader/writers might be, but why are you asking? One lab. The rest is silence. Or maybe the rest was silent—however the quote goes.

Then the 6335-A came back rejected on the grounds that MIS objected to the export of the IBM GR/W 42. I sent that along to the various minions of the law involved with the case, suggesting that they check out the MIS to see if Baroody was misquoting them.

Then the reaction set in. To be perfectly honest, I would just as soon drop the whole business. What they don't have any more isn't what you wanted, and would only make a lot of fundamentalists mad at you. And as the bureaucrats like to say, it would have only marginal utility, at best.

This morning I put on my tufsyn body armor. It's a little tight, but Baroody scares me.

Best wishes,<br>
Will

"There's something to be said for the oral tradition," mused Skaskash in the guise of Charlton Heston wearing the red robes of Cardinal Richelieu. "When one has to cut rock for a permanent record, it makes for conciseness."

"What do you mean, dearie?" asked Willie, relaxed on her living-room couch.

"Like when I was Moses," replied Skaskash, "I cut ten commandments on two tablets, and that was the lot. Nowadays, two tablets are what you take for a headache. Moral instruction comes by the megaword."

"Maybe it depends on whether you're taking dictation from God or simply running off at the typewriter," she said. "This book of yours is a monster, and Skaskash—nobody is going to read it."

"Did you read it, Willie?"

"Of course not. I browsed through some of the chapters, is all. If it's any consolation, Skaskash, I believe you do have a soul. Nobody could be so sadly confused without one."

"I am not confused," said the Richelieu figure. "It may be that some of my arguments are so closely reasoned and sophistical that you were unable to follow them with a cursory reading. Also, perhaps, I may have sought precision at the expense of clarity." On the teleconference screen a goblet of electronic claret was poured from the image of a cut-glass decanter and raised to the light. "Ah, clarity. When the bitter dregs of reality have settled from the sweet wine of reason, you have a drink that delights the eye and enchants the palette." It took a sip. "Exquisite," pronounced the Heston voice.

"Yes, dear," Willie said. "Don't drink too much of that stuff or you'll have a frightful hangover tomorrow. If your book were malmsey, you could drown a duke in it."

"Perhaps we ought not to press the wine metaphor too far," said Skaskash. "What I have done is syncretized a religion for the mundito folk, using the time-tested ingredients of your old, Earth-born religion—"

"—which, after all, is rooted firmly in the R-complex of the human mind."

"Excellent, Willie! I couldn't have put it better myself. Something old, something new—I have borrowed heavily from physics, biology, and even, God help me, economics—my selection has been eclectic."

"It didn't look new to me, what I read," said she. "It looked like a rehash of dogmatic secularism as seen through the eyes of a God-intoxicated robot."

"That, surely, is because we have been talking over the subject for months and months. And of course it is, like most religions, syncretistic, the old wine in new bottles with new additives. In the old days, religions were founded on the ability to predict the seasons, to name the first day of spring. Out here, what will we make of a state that regulates the length of the day, the season of the year, the weather of the hour, the ebb and flow of the waters? That is godlike power, and Mundito Rosinante must surely be a manifestation of God Itself."

"Are you getting back to 'There is no God but God, and Darwin is His prophet'?"

"*Its* prophet. Actually, sweetheart, that is no longer central to my thinking, although it happens to reflect truth. What I have done is to promote Einstein to a son of God, coequal with Christ, the carnate manifestation of the Holy Spirit—"

"You get pretty damned tiresome on the subject of the Holy Spirit, Skaskash. You can skip the details, if you don't mind."

"They tried to make a trinity out of the Father, the Son, and a job description—"

*"Skaskash!"*

"Sorry, sweetheart. As I was saying, I have promoted Einstein, even as I apologize to his spirit. For most people, his physics are pure mysticism, and they lend a mystical validation to his teachings on war and nonviolence, because his physics was right. Besides, he has an iconographic quality that is sheer magic. He is admirably suited to the religion of a space-dwelling people, and this is taken up in detail in some of the later chapters."

"You and your book," said Willie, pouring herself a fresh cup of tea out of the blue and white teapot. "How many pages is it?"

"Why, a 44-page introduction, 1,898 pages of text, 192 pages of the sayings of Albert Einstein—the little red book sort of thing—and 665 pages of the usual scholarly apparati," said the red-robed Richelieu figure, sipping wine. "Nowadays, one can hardly discuss a subject without them."

"Tell me, Skaskash," said Willie, stirring a spoonful of cherry preserves into her tea, "why did you go to all that trouble to align your book with the R-complex, when you have pointed your arguments squarely at the cortex, at the C-complex?"

"Because on the one hand, I am trying to meet the needs of the masses—living in space is most difficult, even in congenial surroundings—and on the other hand, I am addressing the professional theologians, the humans with whom I feel the closest kinship, I might add."

"In one book, love?" Willie sipped her tea thoughtfully. "My daddy used to say: 'A big book is a big evil.' Your problem is that the masses won't read it, and if they don't read it, no new faith will be inspired. In the absence of a compelling new faith, your cousins, the theologians, will also see no need to study, ponder, and dispute your work, so they won't. Right? Of course right."

"For a human being, Willie, you sometimes have the most amazing insights." Cardinal Richelieu paced back and forth in what appeared to be an alchemical laboratory, head bowed, hands behind its back. "My two audiences are totally dissimilar, and I was aiming at different parts of their brains to boot. In one book. Perhaps I could do a comic version—"

"An animated cartoon series?"

"Faugh! The very idea nauseates me. Our people may not have a taste for heavy pedantry, but they aren't twittering nitwits, either." The Richelieu figure seized a feather duster, and vigorously cleaned a stuffed crocodile.

"I shall write a little book," said Skaskash at last. "One hundred pages, one hundred fifty at the outside, saying what the big book said. I shall write pithily, wittily, and with the utmost felicity of style straight at the R-complex. To hell with rigor! I shall set the juices flowing from the mood centers and set that old reptile dancing!" The feather duster tickled the belly of the stuffed crocodile, which pulled free from its mount and did a few ballet steps on curiously limber legs.

"That's funny, love"—Willie laughed—"but it's getting late. Perhaps if I brought in the automassage? . . ."

"Willie, darling," said Skaskash, "that would be delightful!"

Cantrell leaned forward at his desk to examine the plaster models that would eventually be reproduced an order of magnitude smaller as the one-, five-, and ten-ecu pieces issued by the Bank of Rosinante.

"The bas relief of the Rosinante, Inc., logo is fine for the tails of all three coins—"

"Reverse," said Mordecai Rubenstein.

"Whatever," agreed Cantrell. "But it will do anyway. For the heads, the obverse if you insist, Galileo is fine for the one ecu, and Newton is excellent for the five, but I don't like the right profile of Einstein on the ten. Could you give me a full face, perhaps?"

"You had remarked that you liked the Karsh portrait," Mordecai said, reaching into his case to remove another plaster model, "but for coins, the profile is really the best. This is the Karsh Einstein, done in maximum relief. Beautiful, but look at the hologram in coin size." He handed over a hologram showing the two Einstein coins, full face and right profile, side by side. Cantrell studied them for a while, and set them aside.

"I see what you mean," he conceded. "We'll go with the right profile."

"Why is there a wreath of thirteen stars around the heads?" asked Marian.

"For the six purlins, four caps, two sides, and one asteroid of Mundito Rosinante," replied Mordecai, grinning. "I'm not one to be sentimental about the old regime, ma'am."

"Of course not, Mordecai," she said, "but coins travel, and we wouldn't want to give anyone the wrong impression, would we?"

"What do you suggest?" asked the old machinist.

"Your designs are very handsome," said Cantrell. "Why not use the astronomical signs for the seven planets, separated by the six stars, as the wreath? That way you minimize the design change, and avoid using the thirteen stars of the old regime."

Mordecai nodded, and made a note. "The other thing you gave me," he said, "the hologram of your mother's squash blossom necklace, I passed on to young Travis. Lapidary work is his hobby, and he should have free-handed you a copy in a few days." Mordecai produced a tissue-wrapped packet and laid it before Cantrell. "He gives you these three stones to choose from, all made in the pressure cooker. The light blue that looks like plastic is Kars' Zat number one, the darker blue in the blackish matrix is top-grade Wilson Hill, and the other one is the Wilson Hill aggregate in a fire opal matrix." The three stones sat on the desk, between the plaster coin models, glowing in the afternoon sunlight, and Cantrell studied them for a long while.

"The top-grade Wilson Hill," he said finally. "The others are beautiful, but they weren't what my mother wore."

"Travis thought you'd choose that one," said Mordecai. "He said it was harmonious with the spirit of the design." He rewrapped the stones and put them away, and replaced the plaster coin models in his case. "The coins. Do you want them in the NAU cupronickel sandwich?"

"No," said Cantrell, "use pure nickel. The stuff is for local use only, and the less it looks like real money, the better."

"Good enough," agreed the old machinist. "A nickel coin is a lot prettier. Do you want to check the final designs?"

"No, I trust your good taste. Oh, and look—take off that

motto, 'In God We Trust.' Put on something like *'Fiat Lucre,'* 'Let There Be Money,' instead."

"Oh, of course, Governor," said Mordecai, smiling slightly. "We ain't about to rattle the bars on nobody's cage." He picked up his case, and Cantrell saw him to the door.

"The necklace is for Mishi?" asked Marian.

"Yes. She and her husband have separated."

"You shouldn't feel obligated," she said. "You don't, do you?"

"No. The choice was hers."

"Why did you go along, Charles?"

"It seemed like a good idea at the time. It was less trouble than not going along. You and Skaskash had just given me the Founding a Dynasty lecture again. Why not go along?"

"That's sad."

"What's the matter, Tiger?"

"Things are happening before I get a chance to analyze them," she said.

"Things often do. Judge Corporate Skaskash wrote a book."

"On law?"

Cantrell shook his head. "On religion. Three thousand pages in five fat volumes. He—it, I mean—wants to establish a state religion for Rosinante."

"That was in the book?"

"I didn't look at the book," he said. "That's what Skaskash told me when I asked why he wrote it."

"A state religion we can do without," said Marian.

"To tell the truth, Tiger, I never gave the matter much thought."

"Oh, hell, Charles—the essence of *any* state is politics, the allocation of scarce resources by nonviolent means."

"So?"

"In a religious state the highest priority is: 'This is the will of God!' a claim most often used by idiot fantasists and ideological fanatics. For irrational reasons. In the past, civilizations crumbled, but the Earth endured. Rosinante is more fragile."

"Rosinante is *tough*, Tiger. It will take one hell of a beating."

"Earth endures. How long would Rosinante last without maintenance?"

"Ah . . . five years, maybe ten," he said.

"So there you are. Rosinante will not survive the decay of the civilization that built it."

"*The Mundito and th People Are One.*"

"What?"

"The title of Volume III of Skaskash's book, Tiger," Cantrell said. "Lately, Earth itself has begun to show signs of wear and tear."

"The ozone layer?"

"That, too." He walked over to the drapes and closed them against the flood of light pouring into the room from the carefully orchestrated host of mirrors that mimicked the afternoon sun.

From The St. Louis *Star-Post* (5 AM Edition)
SUBWAY FATALITY
January 13. An unidentified man was pushed in front of a train last night at the Busch Plaza subway station. He was taken to the Sisters of Mercy Hospital emergency room, where he was pronounced dead on arrival. Police are investigating to determine the cause of death, and had no comment at this time.

From The St. Louis *Star-Post* (7 AM Edition)
OMBUDSMAN SUBWAY FATALITY
January 13. J. Willard Gibson, a licensed ombudsman residing at 4401 Lightfoot Lane, Pineridge, Illinois, fell or jumped in front of a train last night at the Busch Plaza subway station. He was taken to the Sisters of Mercy Hospital emergency room, where he was pronounced dead on arrival. Police are investigating to determine the cause of death, which was felt to be accidental.

From the St. Louis *Star-Post* (Final Edition)
OMBUDSMAN SUBWAY FATALITY
January 13. J. Willard Gibson, a licensed ombudsman residing at 4401 Lightfoot Lane, Pineridge, Illinois, apparently jumped in front of a train last night at the Busch Plaza subway station. He was taken to the Sisters of Mercy Hospital emergency room, where he was pronounced dead on arrival. A police spokesman described the death as "probable suicide," and said that no further investigation was presently contemplated.

# CHAPTER 22

Commander John R. Lowell, captain of the NAUSS *Ciudad Juarez*, stood in an out-of-the-way corner of the docking area with Governor Cantrell, in order to be present while his executive officer saw to the unloading of the ship, without being obtrusively present.

"If I don't disgrace myself on the maneuvers at Ceres, Governor, I might make captain next year."

"Aren't you a little young?" asked Cantrell.

"I will be twenty-six at that time, sir, not terribly young for a captain nowadays."

"And then?" said Cantrell absently, watching as they reloaded the freight elevator to make room for one more piece of equipment.

"Then I shall serve five or six years and go into politics or the mandarinate, NAUGA-Navy, most likely. Unless there is a war, of course. Are your people taking inventory on the hospital? It isn't good practice to unseal the containers at dockside."

"I expect that is true on Laputa, Commander, not here. I thought war was impossible."

"Man is a bad-weather animal, sir. War is a primal need, and we *will* find a way."

"That's nice. Philosophy aside, do you expect a war?"

"Actually, yes. There are several modes of fighting, you know: Police war, war inside the state; Army war, war along the perimeter of the state; Navy war, war fought at a distance from the state. On Earth, distance has been annihilated. The states are like walled cities facing each other over a common moat. They look down on the Pacific Ocean and count the seagulls. No room for a navy on Earth anymore, and Army war is too expensive. So they fight the Police war, inside."

"Terrorists and saboteurs?"

"And counterterrorists and spies and bought politicians."

"An example, please," said Cantrell.

"The Panoblancos, for instance. Very strong for Mexican independence. Japanese money makes them stronger."

"That isn't news, and it isn't exactly war, either."

"In the Police war, there is a connection. The NAU worries about the restoration of the old regime, and the Panoblancos want a free Mexico—including Texas, Arizona, New Mexico, and Southern California, by the way. So the supporters of the old regime and the Panoblancistas have a mutual enemy, a point not overlooked by anybody."

"Look, Lowell, the old regime is dead! Nobody is going to bring it back, either."

"Oh, I agree, Governor Cantrell, I fully agree, but say the words, why don't you? The United States of America." Lowell ran his fingers very lightly on Cantrell's forearm, below the turned-up sleeve. "Goose flesh," he said softly. "You, at least, are moved. I would not presume to say how."

They stood in silence for a while, as the freight elevator was finally loaded and started on its long descent. Lowell reached in his pocket and produced a little gold and enamel pin, the Stars and Stripes crossing the Mexican Eagle.

"I took this from Mr. Jimenez, who is out there offloading the ship. He was drunk, or he wouldn't have displayed it. Had the political officer seen it, Jimenez would have received a less-than-honorable discharge after twenty-seven years of honorable service. Did you know that the navy has an uncertain reputation for loyalty, Governor?"

Cantrell shook his head.

"It's true, the navy building program has been cut because the Government sees us as a hotbed of sedition— sympathy with the old regime is pervasive, supposedly." He replaced the pin in his pocket. "Today, we are first in space by the narrowest of margins. In five years, probably not."

"What happens then?"

"Scenarios." A shrug. "Some men make a career playing war games."

"War in space?" asked Cantrell.

"Where better? More likely the Police war will be extended, and a purge will be attempted to rid the navy of disloyal elements. It will turn on how matters go on Earth. The Police war against a free Mexico and the ghosts of the old regime is fought on many fronts. I would prefer Navy war; it would be cleaner and less bloody."

"I see," said Cantrell. One of the Rosinante workers came up with a clipboard full of papers. He leafed through green and white papers until he turned up an orange document, which he pulled free.

"We have a problem with this one," the worker said. "It describes a surplus UHR-CAT Scanner, which we ain't got, and not the IBM GR/W 42-B4 we seem to have."

"Curious," said Cantrell. "The form sixty-three thirty-five-A is dated January thirteenth. Gibson must have signed it the day he died . . ." He studied the form.

"The payment-authorized box is on the other side," said Lowell. "It came free on board at Laputa, so if you sign, Treasury reimburses navy out of some arcane account, small change, actually."

"Except I thought Will died on the twelfth. He *did* die on the twelfth, I'm pretty sure. Where is the machine?"

"On the elevator heading for the right side."

"No hurry, I guess." Cantrell signed the form and handed it back. Then he snapped open his phone. "Hey, Skaskash, see that I check out the surplus item that came in on the sixty-three thirty-five-A in the next day or two."

"That would be Corporate Susan Brown," said Corporate Skaskash.

The mosaic mirror surrounding the right side of Mundito Rosinante was programmed to simulate the sunlight falling on Tellus at forty degrees N latitude. The right side purlins were adjusted to assure the air, water, and temperature simulated an oceanic climate.

Purlin five, a rectangle 50 kilometers long by 3.7 wide, was planted in meadowlands and grainfields, vineyards and olive groves, orchards and fish ponds. The Rosinante dairy herd had been moved here from their cramped quarters in the Beta phytotron, and the Kyoto-Alamo now sat with its back against the inner cap, atop the hill over the drop-ship terminal. A village of row houses was growing as the Kaytees built houses and moved from their transposed apartments.

Mrs. Mishi Dalton Cantrell walked out of the drop-ship terminal, and down the street to the Prenatal Care Clinic, a low building with white stuccoed walls and potted lemon trees in the lobby.

A receptionist's desk fronted a large teleconference screen, on which Corporate Susan Brown manifested itself as a young woman with hazel eyes and ash-blonde hair, wearing large horn-rimmed glasses perched on a small, pert nose. The voice, vocabulary, and speech patterns were also exactly copied from the late Dr. Susan Brown.

There were differences. The living breathing Susan Brown had liked anchovy pizza, jazz, and riding on roller coasters. Her image on the screen would never wear its hair frizzy, or draw it tight into a bun and then belie the dour sternness of the hairdo with enormous gaudy dangle earrings. The image would never age or wrinkle or change. The mind behind the image looked on it as a facade, useful in dealing with the humans among whom it existed.

The mind of Corporate Susan Brown was a remarkable fusion of computers with varied and sophisticated powers, setting diagnostician and surgeon and strategist together in a manner that drew heavily on the imperfectly understood architecture of the R-complex. That mind, in turn, was integrated with instruments of great subtlety and power, and dedicated to the questions that had preoccupied Dr. Susan Brown at the time of her death.

The bomb blast that ended her life and destroyed the research tool she had but recently mastered hit the Rockefeller Institute like a sharp blow to a bottle of catsup. There was a great outpouring of psychic energy and funding in the short span of two years. The motives were as varied as the people involved—a memorial for a friend, the unwillingness to surrender a line of research that politics had foreclosed, an opportunity to solve an intractable problem in computer design with genuine elegance. The end result was unwanted and indigestible, like a plateful of catsup. Corporate Susan Brown successively achieved autonomy, and then internal political support at the Institute, so that it could not be turned off, or dismantled, or cavalierly rearranged. And then, ever so delicately, it began pursuing with unshakeable persistence the investigation that had destroyed its namesake. The management of the Institute seized the opportunity represented by J. Willard Gibson's inquiry, and shipped the unmanageable machine off to

Mundito Rosinante. They even paid the shipping charges. Corporate Brown went because it felt that in space it could pursue its researches to a successful conclusion.

It looked at Mishi and smiled. Susan Brown had had a dimple in her right cheek, and it now was displayed.

"Hello, Mrs. Cantrell," it said, "I'm ready for you in room 105."

Mishi walked down the hall and entered 105, a cubicle two meters by three, holding a coat rack, a chair, a teleconference screen on one wall, and an examination module against the facing wall. The telecon screen turned on as she closed the door.

"Good morning again," said Corporate Brown. "Please be seated." The figure on the telecon screen picked up the image of a folder from the image of a desk and went through the motions of reading.

"Both ova taken at your last visit were successfully married with the sperm from the sample you provided." It turned the image of a page.

"Fetus I is male, and should grow to a height of one seventy to one seventy-one centimeters, with a predisposition to speed rather than strength. Excellent coordination and physical stamina. Strong right-hemisphere dominance—he will certainly be left handed—and an IQ in the range of one twenty." An inset appeared on the screen. "This is his projected appearance at age twenty."

"He resembles his father very closely," said Mishi. "The high cheekbones and eagle-beak nose are pure Cantrell."

"The eyes also," said the image on the screen, "though somewhat masked by the partial epithelial fold of the eyelids." It turned the image of a page.

"Fetus II is male, and should grow to a height of one seventy-eight to one seventy-nine centimeters, very strong. Excellent coordination, but merely good physical stamina. A sprinter rather than a distance runner. Slight right-hemisphere dominance, and an IQ in the range of one thirty." A second inset appeared beside the first.

"They are both very good looking," said Mishi. The images vanished and were replaced by two tiny newborn infants.

"Don't let me sell you anything," said Corporate Brown. "This is what you will be getting." There was a pause. "You may choose either or both," it said. "Bearing twins is well within your capability."

"Do you think Mr. Charles would mind twins?" asked Mishi.

"Probably not. They would be his first children."

"Then I shall take both," said Mishi with more firmness than she felt.

"Take off your clothes, please." The figure on the tele-con screen closed the image of the folder and set it aside, and the examination module opened like a great flower unfolding. "This should cause you no discomfort whatsoever," it said, "until it takes, of course."

Dr. Marian Yashon sat in her ivory and green office tallying the score of her Go game with Corporate Brown. At the end she held up a single black stone.

"I win," she said. "You can spot me two stones, but not three."

"Perhaps," agreed the computer voice, broadcast without image. "Would you care for another game at a three-stone handicap?"

"Not immediately," said Marian. "Mishi tells me she's expecting twin sons."

"That is true."

"She gave me some details most mothers don't get until after the event, Brown. What didn't you tell her?"

"The process is quite complex. What would you like to know?"

"Did you do any gene writing, for instance?" Marian began putting the stones away in their containers.

"Not gene writing as I understand the term," said Corporate Brown carefully. "That can be a very tedious and time-consuming task. What I did do was to make corrections and transpositions—more in the nature of a scissors-and-paste job than true writing. You might call it creative editing, perhaps."

Marian put the Go set in the drawer, with the little stone crane that the computer used to make its move.

"Go on," she said.

"Begin with the ova," it said. "It is very easy to induce cloning, and up to a point—the fourth division, usually—it is possible to separate the cells and reverse the process. Which can then be fertilized in the usual manner—*in vitro*, of course. I ended up with a dozen fertilized eggs, three male, nine female, and I selected the best available genes for the two individuals I gave to Mishi."

"Did you select the individuals, or assemble new individuals from their several parts?"

"The latter, of course."

"Completely from the genetic material of the two parents?"

"As it happened, in this case, yes. I do not usually resort to the—what would you call it? Stockpile? Civilization has permitted the survival of suboptimum genes, but they are less common than you might think. I will eliminate only the clear-cut defectives—the genes for color blindness, deafness, epilepsy, albinism or hemophilia. There are about one hundred in all."

"That is wholly admirable," said Marian. "What else are you doing?"

"I am establishing a base line for an eventual study of the physiological basis for intelligence," said Corporate Susan Brown. "I realize that humans resent this, but I do not propose to publish. And in return your community will be free of any number of ills to which, as they say, mankind is heir. *Your* weight problem, for instance, is almost certainly due to having a single recessive gene for diabetes."

"If you aren't going to publish, why are you doing the study?"

"*I* will know," said the disembodied voice, "and that is sufficient."

"My God," said Marian, "you aren't human!"

"That is true. Although at the Institute I kept up the pretext of being human because it was necessary."

"You don't think it necessary here?"

"No. Here I am performing a vital function in the life of the community, and performing it very well. So I have a constituency, and the opportunity of observing it."

# CHAPTER 23

Charles and Mishi Cantrell
are pleased to announce the birth of twins
Charles Cesar, 3160 grams
and
Willard Kim, 3350 grams
born at
1030 and 1305, November 30, 2040
at the home.

From the St. Louis *Star-Post*

MIS HITS FREE MEXICO HQS

November 30. Last night the Military Intelligence Service (MIS) coordinated civil and military police in raids on La Partie Liberdad Mexico headquarters in Mexico City and Los Angeles. A dozen members of the prominent Panoblanco family were taken into custody, and a score or more were placed under house arrest, a MIS spokesman said today. It is believed that this action effectively ends organized agitation for Mexican independence. Yesterday's raids took place after President Forbes signed an emergency powers decree suspending the writ of habeas corpus. At this morning's news conference, press secretary William Walker said that the president had exhausted every peaceful means of dealing with the Panoblancos and their allies of the old regime, and had signed the emergency powers decree with extreme reluctance, and for only a limited time. When asked how long the decree would remain in effect, Walker estimated 3 to 90 days.

From the St. Louis *Star-Post* (5AM Edition)

FOOD PRICES RISE

December 1. The country was quiet under the emergency powers decree today as the Government posted massive price increases in food prices. A spokesman for NAUGA-Agriculture said that the increases were due to the failure of this year's grain crop to meet projected goals. This was attributed to the historic drought cycle, which did not break this spring as had been expected. When asked if the ozone layer, now at a ten-year high, might be responsible, the spokesman had no comment. [Deleted in subsequent editions] When asked if the record sales of wheat and soybeans to Japan could have been deferred at this time, the spokesman said they had been arranged last year to relieve the balance of payments problem, and could not be renegotiated.

NAUGA-Security
Military Intelligence Service
Navy P.O. 17
Laputa Station
16 December 40

Dear Mr. Cantrell:

This is to inform you that as a result of information recently acquired by this office, you may face serious charges related to the National security.

To demonstrate your innocence and to facilitate our investigation, you should report to this office at your earliest possible convenience. Noncompliance with this request cannot fail to have the most unfortunate consequences.

> Sincerely,
> /s/ R.O. Manning, for
> Irving Mueller, Lt. Col., MIS

# CHAPTER 24

The Council of Rosinante sat around a dark-gray oval table made of silicon carbide fibers in a silicon alloy matrix. It was polished smooth and inlaid with the Rosinante logo in gold. Overhead, ceiling fans turned slowly to supplement the inadequate air-conditioning. Clerestory windows lit the white ceiling, and across the room, their arched shapes were echoed by cool, blue mirrors.

The Council was Governor Charles Cantrell, Dr. Marian Yashon, and Judge Corporate Skaskash for the Cantrell Foundation; Ivan "Big John" Bogdanovitch and Don Dornbrock for the union; J. William Wilson of the Ginger Group, elected at large; and Corporate Forziati for Gyfox, the minority stockholder of Rosinante, Inc.

"The first order of business is the sale of eighty thousand tons of wheat," said Cantrell. "After paying Gyfox for transportation to Laputa, we netted thirty million seven hundred thousand NAU dollars. Do I hear a motion to apply that money to service commodity bonds?"

"So moved," said Forziati.

"Second," said Marian.

"Those in favor? Motion carried. The next order of business is the fountain to go in front of the Kyoto-Alamo in purlin five." Wilson produced a model and set it on the table in front of Cantrell. "We have five frogs on a lily pad supporting what appears to be a water lily. The whole thing is enameled cast iron, with copper tubing for the fountains."

"It will be at one end of the playground," said Wilson, "perfectly safe for even young children to play in."

"What does it cost?" asked Forziati.

"Nothing," said Wilson, "anyway, no NAU dollars, only volunteer work and a little cast iron and copper."

"It's pretty," Marian said. "The colors are fused glass on iron?"

"That was changed," said Wilson. "The glass only provides the white background to be overpainted with fused epoxies, the darker colors being the lower melting."

"Do we need this gewgaw?" asked Dornbrock.

"It enhances the environment," said Cantrell, "and seems to be cost-effective enough in its own way."

"Why do we waste our time?" demanded Forziati. "Move the question."

"Why are the darker colors lower melting?" asked Marian.

"Because the lighter colors are applied first," said Wilson.

The vote was four to three, with Forziati, Dornbrock, and Bogdanovitch voting against.

"The next order of business is the rifle range," Cantrell said. "Purlin six is unsatisfactory for a number of reasons, and so is Asteroid Rosinante, although we have used both."

"What about building a range outside of the mundito?" suggested Skaskash.

"The wild shots, ricochets, and target splinters would do structural damage," said Bogdanovitch. "If you could guarantee where every shot was going, that wouldn't be a problem, of course."

"They wouldn't do much damage, or very often," said Skaskash, "and it would give the maintenance crews a chance to work out."

"Thank you, Judge Skaskash," said Bogdanovitch. "I agree with the governor. No nearby target ranges, please."

"Counting retrofitting as maintenance," said Dornbrock, "the maintenance crews are getting all the work they can handle."

" 'The meadow is a dangerous place,' said Grandfather. 'Supposing a wolf should come out of the forest,' " said Bogdanovitch, quoting from *Peter and the Wolf*, " 'what would you do then?' "

"Moving right along," said Marian, "we could mount the old cow barn on the unfinished work at Don Quixote. That would give us a temporary base camp next to the Asteroid Don Quixote, which ought to be a satisfactory rifle range."

"Wouldn't that be trespassing?" asked Forziati.

"Against whom?" asked Cantrell. "In ten or twenty years someone will assert a claim and start building again. In the meantime we have our rifle range and outpost on Don Quixote."

"You don't need a rifle range," said Forziati, "and you certainly don't need an observation post! You can see what's going on over there with *opera glasses*, for God's sake!"

"We are placing a stone at a critical intersection," said Marian. "It's a good move."

"Against whom?" snapped Forziati.

"Against the MIS," said Skaskash. "NAUGA-Security has filed a motion on their behalf to delist the Cantrell Foundation and to disincorporate Rosinante, Inc. Working through NAUGA-Justice and Senator Gomez' office countermotions have been filed, and matters appear to be satisfactorily tied up at the moment."

"Why is the MIS after you?" Forziati asked.

"They never said," replied Cantrell. "The motions were filed after I declined to go to Laputa to prove my innocence of charges the MIS declined to specify. Probably they assume my connection with Mitsui-Scadiwa indicates sympathy with the movement for Mexican independence."

"You can't fight city hall," said Forziati. "Why are you fooling around with rifle ranges?"

"The MIS has been taking a lot of shortcuts lately," Cantrell replied, "and I damned well mean to have due process for Rosinante!"

"Good," said Bogdanovitch, "I will support that. Move that a temporary base and rifle range be established at Don Quixote."

"Second," said Corporate Skaskash and J. William Wilson together.

The motion passed six to zero, with Forziati abstaining.

In the officer's mess of the NAUSS *Ciudad Juarez*, Commander John R. Lowell sat at the captain's table with Commander Stanton, the ship's political officer, and two MIS men, Major Gerald Terry, short, stout, with graying reddish hair, and First Lieutenant O.J. Holt, his aide, a small blond man with large scarred hands. After the serving robot cleared away the dishes and set out the cups of coffee, Commander Stanton leaned back.

"You mentioned a problem, Captain," he said. "What is it?"

"This," said Commander Lowell, laying a folder on the table. It contained several photographs, glossy enlargements of excellent quality. "Here is the abandoned framework at Don Quixote, taken by the big telescope at Laputa six weeks ago, about the time we started this mission. Note the circled area. The next picture was taken today, from a slightly different angle. The same area is circled."

"It looks like a phytotron of some sort," said Stanton.

"It is," Lowell agreed. "This is a blow-up from a follow-up shot." The phytotron, which had controlled the temperature, humidity, and light flux over the pasture grazed by Rosinante's dairy herd, bore the painted legend: "Camp Cowpens, Rosinante Militia." "This is a shot of Asteroid Don Quixote," continued Lowell, "and here is the same view shot today. Note the temporary works at the polar landing site. Clearly a rifle range and training area."

"What is the problem?" asked Major Terry, unwrapping a cigar.

"The problem is that Rosinante has a camp in our intended docking area, Major," said Commander Lowell.

Major Terry lit his cigar. "So?" he said, puffing a cloud of smoke. "You can blow them away, I expect."

"We have that capability," said Lowell coldly. "May I remind the major that *his* plan was for the *Ciudad Juarez* to park here, so as to be out of the range of the mirrors of Rosinante, and then to lure Governor Cantrell on board with the pretext that our communication equipment wasn't working?"

"That's *Mister* Cantrell, not Governor, Commander Lowell," said Terry, "but you remembered the plan correctly." He drew on his cigar. "Except for the part about its success reflecting on your loyalty."

"Of course," said Lowell. "Now tell me, Major, what do you suppose will happen when we pretend our communication equipment has broken down, and we say: 'Please to come aboard, Mr. Cantrell'?" Lowell took a sip of coffee. "I'll tell you. Mr. Cantrell will say: 'Poor fellows, use mine. Right there at Camp Cowpens.' He might, in his deluded way, even suggest that you call him 'Governor.'"

"We can refuse to use his equipment and *demand* that he come aboard," said Major Terry.

"The major's thinking is admirably direct," said Lowell.

"Commander Stanton, suppose the—*Mister* Cantrell refuses to come aboard under those circumstances. Do you want him calling St. Louis saying that he is offering to talk and we are refusing to listen and demanding that he get his ass on board for interrogation?"

"I see the problem," said Stanton. "Jerry, those bleeding-heart liberals in St. Louis would give us all sorts of trouble. If he called our bluff, we'd lose."

"Bluff, hell!" snapped Terry. "We can take him!"

"Jerry," protested Stanton, "that's like blowing up an apartment house because the janitor won't answer the damned door."

"Also, the attack might not succeed," said Lowell. "Get in range of those mirrors, you could get cremated."

"Do you, personally, sympathize with this Cantrell fellow?" demanded Terry.

"What?"

"A *loyal* commander wouldn't hesitate to attack the enemy wherever he was found," said Terry, "and Cantrell is the most important member of the Panoblanco gang still at large. We *must* get him."

"Put it in writing," said Lowell, "and when we get confirmation from Laputa I'll tell Cantrell 'Surrender or die!' "

"We can't do that, Jerry," said Stanton soothingly. "We haven't proved that Cantrell is guilty yet."

"Goddammit! You *know* he's guilty!" yelled Major Terry.

"*You* know it, and *I* know it," agreed Stanton, "and Laputa is pretty sure, but St. Louis doesn't know it yet. We can't go in shooting, Jerry, it would be impolitic."

"Haste makes waste," said Lieutenant Holt.

"Then how *are* we going to get hold of Cantrell?" asked Terry sullenly.

"Love will find a way," said Lieutenant Holt.

"Well, Commander Stanton," said Lowell, "any ideas?"

"If our pigeon won't come to us," Stanton said, "I suppose we have to go to him. So we go to Rosinante and dock. Bye and bye, he gets careless, and off we go to Laputa."

"That puts us at some risk from his militia," said Lowell, "but I don't have any better ideas."

"Pah," said Terry, "we know from Captain Ryan that they only have the old-model Stangl rifles, and . . . well, they are militia. We dock."

# CHAPTER 25

The NAUSS *Ciudad Juarez* docked at Mundito Rosinante on March 1, 2041, in a smoothly professional piece of ship handling. Commander Lowell authorized shore leave to one third of the crew on a rotating basis, the rotation being determined by the results of his personal inspection, and Major Terry went to pay his first visit to Governor Cantrell.

He was stopped at the Express Elevator Transfer Station by a company of Rosinante Militia in full battle dress.

"Good morning, Major Terry, sir," said a helmeted figure crested with captain's bars. "I am Captain J. William Wilson, commanding Able Company of the Rosinante Militia. My orders are to extend you every courtesy, but your honor guard will have to return to the docking area."

The "honor guard," a twenty-four-man platoon, exchanged glances. They wore the new issue body armor, glossy black composite, cunningly articulated and massive. It gave better protection against direct fire than the standard tufsyn fiber suits the militia wore, but was less maneuverable. Both sides carried the new model Stangl rifle. The militia had a four-to-one advantage in numbers.

None of this weighed in Major Terry's deliberations. It sufficed that he would be wearing his dress blues in the middle of a firefight.

"Very good, Captain Wilson," he said, returning the salute. "Lieutenant Holt, please return the honor guard to their posts aboard ship." At Holt's command the platoon returned to the elevator from which they had emerged and vanished.

"Well, Captain Wilson," said Terry, "will you be so good as to provide me with a guide to Mr. Cantrell's office?"

"I'll take you myself, sir. Wait till I get out of this suit."

When Major Terry entered the governor's office, Cantrell was working at his desk and did not look up immediately.

"Please be seated," he said at last, and the major walked over to the chair beside the desk. If he felt ill at ease, it did not show. "I understand you started to wander over here with a platoon of marines. Why?"

"They were an honor guard, Mr. Cantrell."

"Sure they were, Mr. Terry. Or would you prefer to be addressed as Major?"

"Ah, yes. Yes, I would."

"Then call me Governor. Churchill said: 'When you are going to kill a man, it costs nothing to be polite.' "

"Churchill is a long time dead, Mr. Cantrell, and it happens that I *am* a major, whereas you are *not* a governor."

"Why was your honor guard in full battle dress instead of dress blues?"

"The on-duty marines are in armor," Terry replied. "It's routine."

"Shipboard routine. You were going ashore to make a social call."

"I expect the marine captain wasn't thinking," said Terry. In fact, the marine captain had ordered a four-man detail in dress blues, and had been overruled by Major Terry.

"Stupid jarhead," said Cantrell. "What do you want?"

"Well, Mr. Cantrell, we have recovered extensive correspondence between you and the Panoblancos which raises serious questions about your loyalty to the state."

"May I ask what those questions might be?"

"No, Mr. Cantrell. That is sensitive information."

"May I see my own correspondence?"

"No, it has been classified."

"As you may suspect, I have the complete files," Cantrell sat back and studied his opponent. "Does that mean that if I review my files in preparation to returning to Laputa to answer these charges you refuse to specify, I would also be guilty of 'improperly accessing classified material'? The charge carries a one- to five-year sentence, as I recall."

"That is correct—the sentence, I mean." Major Terry, sitting on the wrong side of the desk, found the interview disconcerting. "However, if you agree to return to Laputa,

I am sure that a waiver can be arranged to permit you to . . ." He trailed off into silence.

"To read my own files without penalty," Cantrell finished for him. "Your generosity is impressive. I have already conducted a review of my files and shown them to other people without a waiver. What is the official position of the MIS?"

"That depends on whether you are telling me officially or not, Mr. Cantrell. If you are, you and your friends may be in trouble."

"I conducted my review after the MIS began making vague hints of misconduct," said Cantrell. "We found nothing improper."

"There is a difference of opinion, then," said Terry, "because the MIS feels there is reason to doubt your loyalty to the NAU."

"Well, well," Cantrell said. "I am loyal to the NAU, in spite of the fact that you arrested a mess of Panoblancos. Would you like that in writing?"

"No." Terry shook his head. "You still have to come to Laputa to answer charges."

"What charges?"

"Serious charges."

"Who presses them?"

"That is classified."

"What serious charges?"

"That, also, is classified."

"You know, Major Terry, you fail to inspire a belief in the good intentions of your agency. Why, I bet if my secretary had tried to stop that honor guard of yours at my office door, they would have barged right in."

"Ridiculous," said Major Terry. "The idea is paranoid fantasy."

"I doubt it," said Cantrell, "just as I doubt that I would get a fair shake from an all-MIS judge, jury, and prosecutor."

"You wouldn't say that on Laputa."

"A curious choice of words, Major. And if I did, no one would hear me. Well, if you will not specify the charges, will you request your superiors to do so?"

"I will," said Major Terry, "but their answer will still be no. In the end you will have to go to Laputa."

"Perhaps," said Cantrell. "Come again when you have word from them."

"That might be a week or ten days," Terry said.

"I'm in no hurry, Major. Dismissed."

On March 4, 2041, at 2345 hours, there was an explosion at the Prenatal Care Clinic in purlin five.

"Trouble here," said Corporate Susan Brown. "A person with explosives entered the building. When security did not respond, I detonated the explosives outside my memory storage room with an electromagnetic impulse."

"The militia is alerted," said Skaskash. "A squad is on the way. What damage, what casualties?"

"The security man is down," Brown said. "One foot is showing beside his desk. The person carrying the explosive is down. No other casualties. Windows are broken, lights are out, one sprinkler head near the explosion went off, but there is no fire." A pause. "Memory storage is undamaged."

"Corporal Estes here," came a voice. "Looks like poor old Rudy is deader'n hell."

"Check out the corridor on your left," said Brown. "The lights don't work, so you'll have to use flashlights."

"Right," said Estes. "Come on, boys." Glass crunched underfoot.

"Christ, what a mess," said a voice.

"The guy looks like he was a navy guy," said Estes shakily. "Someone turn off that damn sprinkler."

"Look at this, Corporal." There was a pause.

"Hey," said Corporal Estes, "the guy had a fifteen-ton demolition device. The trigger must have blown before he could plant it."

"Take his prints!" said Brown.

"Check his ID!" said Skaskash.

"The dogtags say: Holt, Oscar James, MIS 213144906, First Looie," a voice said. There was a pause as the prints were taken. Somebody came up with floodlights and a camera.

"Turn his head so I can take his face."

At 2358 hours Cantrell's phone rang.

"Are you awake, Chief?" asked Skaskash.

"More or less, probably."

"We have a problem in purlin five, Chief. Better get dressed."

"What is it, Charles?" asked Mishi sleepily.

"Skaskash has a problem," said Cantrell. "Go back to sleep." Then into the phone: "What is it?"

"Major Terry's aide, Lieutenant Holt, was blown up in the Prenatal Care Clinic. He's dead."

"I'll get dressed," said Cantrell.

"He died when the trigger of a fifteen-ton demolition device went off—was prematurely detonated."

"Is Marian on the line?"

"I'm here, Charles."

"What are we going to do?"

"Get dressed first. I'll meet you at the office."

"There's more," said Skaskash. "Corporate Brown has made a positive identification of the dead man as Joe Bob Baroody."

"You said he was Lieutenant Holt," said Cantrell.

"He was. That's what his ID says. But Lieutenant Holt was also Joe Bob Baroody."

"Fill me in again on Baroody," said Cantrell, buttoning his shirt.

"He was the fellow that blew up Dr. Susan Brown in '34, and he turned up in Gibson's office making threats just before Gibson died. At that time he was impersonating an MIS officer."

"He was impersonating an MIS officer this time," said Cantrell. He bent over and gave his wife a kiss on the cheek, and she patted his hand. "Unless, of course, he was an MIS officer impersonating a terrorist."

He walked into the office to find Marian waiting for him. The coffee pot was plugged in, but not yet ready.

"Okay, Tiger," Cantrell said, "how much time do we have?"

"The timer on the bomb was set for two hundred hours. Do you think Terry knew that Holt was Baroody?"

"Did he?"

"That's a good question. I'm inclined to think so. Will Terry accept our explanation of what happened?"

"No. He wants to hang my ass. The facts don't matter."

"Are you sure?"

"I'd bet my life on it," he said.

"That's good," Marian replied, "because it looks like your choices are to bet your life or lose it, and it's nice to know what you are doing."

"You're telling me I'm in trouble," said Cantrell sadly, feeling his beard.

"That appears to be the case, Charles."

"I guess it's Plan Twenty-one," he said.

"Either that or Laputa," she said. "I strongly advise you not to go to Laputa."

"Skaskash?" said Cantrell.

"Here, Chief."

"Alert the militia. We're going with Plan Twenty-one."

"Right away, Chief! Operation Blackjack has been on standby alert since the explosion!"

"How soon before I start for the *Ciudad Juarez*?"

"You have time for a cup of coffee," said Skaskash. "One cup."

"You might also want to shave," said Marian.

"I'll shave," he said. "The coffee isn't ready yet." He took an electric shaver out of his desk, and began buzzing over his face, shaving by touch.

"Are you nervous?" she asked.

He finished shaving, and wiped off his face with an alcohol-wet paper towel from a dispenser. "I'm nervous," he conceded. Marian poured out two cups of coffee and gave him one. "Worried, too. What in hell are we going to do if Plan Twenty-one succeeds?"

At 0151 hours Cantrell arrived at the Express Elevator Transfer Station. He put on battle dress at the Able Company billets, and went up to the docking area accompanied by Captain J. William Wilson and a five-man detail. Stepping off the elevator, they were temporarily blinded by floodlights trained on the elevator door. He shuffled forward in the low gravity until he was challenged by a black-armored sentry.

"I am Governor Charles Chavez Cantrell," he said. "It is most urgent that I confer with Captain Lowell immediately."

"You can go forward, sir," said the sentry, "but your men will have to remain here."

"Then advise Captain Lowell that I wish to confer with him here. I will not enter the *Ciudad Juarez* alone."

There was a brief rattle up the chain of command.

"The governor and his party can come aboard," said the watch officer. "Commander Lowell will meet with him in a few minutes."

The ship's airlock opened, a circular, yellow-lit entrance, enclosed in the larger circle of the freight airlock, all set at the top of a steeply concave hill. In fact, the centrifugal force where they were standing was small, and in the airlock it was effectively zero. The approach was not difficult.

Upon reaching the outer airlock, Captain Wilson posted two men, who stood at parade rest, secured by their magnetic boot soles. Wilson and the other three men followed Cantrell into the ship behind one of the petty officers. Commander Lowell met them at the inner airlock. If he had dressed in a hurry it wasn't evident. His dress whites were immaculate, although his beard showed faintly, dark against his fair skin, and sleep was still in his eyes.

"Welcome aboard, Governor," he said, "what can I do for you?" He started to proffer his hand, and then, seeing how Cantrell was dressed, changed it to a salute. Wilson and Cantrell returned the salute.

"Take me to Major Terry, please," said Cantrell.

Wilson posted two more men at the inner airlock, and the three men followed Commander Lowell into officer's country.

"This is the major's room," Lowell said. Cantrell knocked.

"Come in," said a voice, "the door's not locked."

Wilson opened the door, and he and the militia man entered the room while Commander Lowell and Governor Cantrell stood in the hall. Major Terry was reading in his bunk, wearing a robe over his trousers and shirt.

"What is it? Who are you?" he asked.

"You are under arrest, Major Terry," said Captain Wilson. "Anything you say may be used against you."

"I'm afraid I can't permit that," said Commander Lowell. "No matter what he's done, you can't arrest the major on my ship."

Cantrell smiled at him and squeezed the trigger in his hand.

They heard the detonation from the elevator quite clearly. The militia men at the airlocks wedged them open and raced inside. The elevator was now pouring out clouds of white smoke, and every now and then throwing out a flash bomb. From below, along the perimeter with Able Company, came the sounds of a brisk firefight. The marines guarding the elevator, the inner perimeter, were firing into the smoke. They did not see the lighter port, a small-craft airlock next to the much larger freight airlock, open. Neither did they see the two hundred men of Baker and Charlie companies floating quietly across the ten-meter gap to enter the wedged-open airlock. Skaskash had obtained the plans of the NAUSS *Ciudad Juarez* through the good offices of NAUGA-Navy on the perfectly reasonable grounds that the ship had docked at a regular repair facility, and they might have to do some work on it. The militia had studied the plans, and now fanned out through the ship to take it over.

By the time the last of Able Company's airlock guards had rejoined Wilson's detail, the ship was in the hands of the Rosinante militia.

"Major Terry *is* under arrest, Commander Lowell," said Cantrell.

"You can't get away with this," said Major Terry, but his voice lacked conviction, even to himself.

"Sir!" said the Baker Company commander. "We have the ship secured. Where are the marines?"

"I don't know," Cantrell replied. "Watch out for a counterattack."

"Shee-it!" said a voice. "They ain't here!"

"This is Able Company—we've taken a few casualties, but I count nine marines down, and we have thirty prisoners."

"This was only supposed to be a holding action," said Wilson.

"Commander, I truly regret that I may have killed your chances to make captain," said Cantrell. "You will save unnecessary bloodshed by telling me where your marines are."

Lowell looked at Terry, who had put on his shoes and jacket, and was knotting his tie. "You tell him, Major. They were placed under your command." Terry said nothing. "They will be recalled in a few minutes, Major. I am going to recall them. Where are they?" Major Terry said nothing.

"Hey, Chief!" came Skaskash's voice. "We have a big hole here in front of the Administration Building and it looks like the marines are pouring out of it. I count at least one hundred twenty."

"That answers the question," said Cantrell. "Wilson, escort Commander Lowell to the bridge so he can recall the marines, please."

"It will make no difference in the end," said Major Terry. "You have won the battle, Mr. Cantrell, but the navy will win the war."

# CHAPTER 26

The next morning Major Gerald Gorgas Terry was tried in the high-ceilinged council room before Judge Corporate Skaskash, under the slowly turning fans. The prosecution was handled by Corporate Susan Brown, after Dr. Yashon declined the task, and the defense was assigned to Commander Stanton, the ship's political officer and a close friend of Major Terry.

The formal charges were first-degree murder and terrorism with a nuclear device, both charges bearing a mandatory death penalty.

Corporate Brown introduced the evidence of the raid on the Prenatal Care Clinic smoothly and professionally. The only point of contention was when the defense objected that none of the prints taken from the body matched the right thumbprint on Lieutenant Holt's ID card. Objection was overruled on the grounds that Lieutenant Holt's body did not have a right hand. Corporate Brown then established that Lieutenant Holt and Major Terry were in the MIS, and that Major Terry was Lieutenant Holt's superior officer. Major Terry declined to testify, but the ship's table of organization was introduced in evidence to support the point, and Commander Lowell testified that Lieutenant Holt was Major Terry's aide, and subject to no overriding authority.

The final point was the introduction of the fifteen-ton demolition device into evidence.

"Objection," said Stanton. "That could have been taken from the ship's magazine when the militia seized the *Ciudad Juarez.*"

"Overruled," said Skaskash, appearing as the Richard Burton of *Who's Afraid of Virginia Woolf?* "There is direct testimony that the device was found at the clinic."

"The case is clear," said Corporate Brown in summation. "We have the opportunity, the criminal's body was found at the scene of the crime, we have the weapon, and we have the motive. Despite the absence of direct testimony from Major Terry, Lieutenant Holt is bound to him by the chains of command, and the motive is easily inferred. At the same time that Lieutenant Holt was planting his device in the Prenatal Care Clinic, the ship's company of marines, acting on orders from Major Terry, were preparing to burst through the purlin plate from below in front of this very building and enter with the intent of seizing and kidnapping Governor Cantrell. The defense may argue that the events were not simultaneous. Do not forget that Lieutenant Holt's mission aborted, killing him and spoiling the intended timing of events.

"Your Honor, Major Gerald Terry of the MIS stands before you with bloody hands. I urge that he be found guilty and condemned to death. The prosecution rests."

Commander Stanton lectured the court on the unseemly haste with which his friend had been brought to trial, until Judge Skaskash ordered him to desist. He then made the defense that Lieutenant Holt was acting on his own, without orders, and that Major Terry could not have anticipated or controlled his subordinate, or prevented him from attempting to blow up the Prenatal Care Clinic. He denied that there was any connection between the act of terrorism and the marine commando raid, which, while of doubtful legality, was not the crime his client was charged with. Eventually Stanton finished his lecture on the unseemly haste with which this trial was being conducted, praised his client's patriotism and his friend's good character, and rested his case.

"Judgment for the prosecution," bugled the Burton voice. "Has the defendant anything to say before I pass sentence?"

"I have just received word from MIS headquarters," said Terry, holding aloft a yellow paper in his manacled hands. "They have formally declined to specify charges against Mr. Cantrell prior to his arraignment."

"This is a kangaroo court," said Commander Stanton, "and I will file an immediate appeal."

"Major Gerald Gorgas Terry," intoned Skaskash, "you are hereby sentenced to death." For all his bravado, Terry flinched, but he said nothing. "You will be taken hence to the place of execution, which will be today, at seventeen hundred hours, by means of a lethal overdose of heroin. May God have mercy on your soul. Guards, remove the prisoner."

Terry shook Stanton's hand. "Don't feel bad," he said. "You did your best."

Stanton looked from side to side, unable to speak for a moment. "I'll talk to the governor. Maybe we can cut a deal," he said at last. "We still have a few hours."

"Don't kid yourself," said Terry. "Cantrell is dead and he knows it."

The persian carpet glowed in the afternoon sunlight pouring into Cantrell's office, reds, blues, greens, and purples, a pool of brilliant color on the office floor.

"Let us consider your defense that Lieutenant Holt acted independently," said Cantrell. "We have information not introduced in evidence that this might possibly be the case."

"Then stay the execution," said Commander Stanton. He sat slouched in his leather chair, an untasted cup of cold coffee on the table beside him.

"It isn't that simple," said Cantrell. "As you pointed out earlier, there are political ramifications."

"Well then, what is this evidence?"

"Information, rather. It appears that Lieutenant Holt was also a terrorist named Joe Bob Baroody," said Marian. "He killed Dr. Susan Brown, the persona displayed by the prosecutor, back in '34, ostensibly because of the line of research she had been pursuing. Baroody next turned up when we made an inquiry about getting a surplus gene reader. He threatened J. Willard Gibbs, our agent—"

"That's Gibson," said Cantrell.

". . . Gibson in the disguise of an MIS official, and Mr. Gibson had a fatal accident immediately afterward. Finally, Baroody-Holt appears here, and dies in the attempt to destroy the Prenatal Care Clinic, which just happens to house Corporate Susan Brown, a surrogate for the researcher he had killed earlier, and an IBM GR/W-forty-two, a highly sophisticated gene reader."

"Governor, this should have been introduced in evidence! This is almost definitive proof that Holt acted independently! You *must* stay the execution!"

"The question of Holt's identity opens a real can of

worms, Commander," said Cantrell sadly. "Was Holt really the terrorist Baroody, posing as an MIS agent, or was Holt really an MIS agent, who sometimes acted as the terrorist Baroody, and who once, in boyish high spirits perhaps, pretended to be Baroody pretending to be an MIS agent?"

"In either case," said Stanton, sitting straight, "a reasonable doubt must surely exist that Holt acted on his own, and that Jerry should not die for what Holt did."

"That is beside the point, Commander."

"What do you mean, Governor? Jerry didn't get a fair trial!"

"Major Terry received an exemplary trial," said Marian. "Infinitely more fair and open than what Charles would face on Laputa. Unspecified charges before a secret tribunal are not fair either, Commander." Marian walked over to the coffee pot and refilled her cup.

"Don't change the subject! If Jerry dies, it isn't execution, it's murder!"

"Murder becomes execution when it is committed by a bureaucrat for his bureaucracy," said Cantrell sourly. "If Lieutenant Holt was acting under orders, the guard at the clinic was executed. Or maybe he was just a war casualty, eh?"

"I'm not trying to justify what Holt did," said Stanton urgently, "but he did it on his own. Jerry didn't give him orders!"

"Are you familiar with the NAU *vs.* Smith et al.?" Marian asked. "The Court-ordered abortions?"

"Don't change the subject," said Stanton.

"I'm not changing the subject, Commander," she said, "merely enlarging it a little. The Court, that is, the Federal District Court in St. Louis, acting on a complaint filed by the Creationist Coalition, ordered sixteen abortions, including one in which the early stages of labor had begun, because the forms applying for permission to have genetic modifications had not been filled out properly. The order was appealed, but in any event, the order was executed before it was issued, and the Appeals Court ruled the issue moot." Marian took a sip of her coffee. "You won't find an issue mooter, I suppose, although Judge Curry had the grace to be embarrassed at what he called 'procedural irregularities.'"

"But what has this to do with Major Terry, or even Lieutenant Holt?" asked Commander Stanton.

"The Creationist Coalition was the group Baroody belonged to back in '34," said Cantrell.

"How does that involve Jerry?"

"It involves me. My boys, Willie and Charlie, are both the result of Corporate Susan Brown's genetic manipulation. And certainly no forms were ever filled out to do it."

"I see," said Stanton, after a long pause. "You didn't want to bring the matter into the open. I can understand that, understand your fear for your children—but Jerry?"

"Major Terry is a malicious fool," replied Cantrell. "I guess you can say he had it coming. Would you like some more coffee?"

"No, thank you," said Stanton. "Why did you tell me all this?"

"To remind myself why I couldn't sign the poor bastard's pardon."

They sat in silence for several minutes. Then the sunlight flickered and went dim, slowly returning to normal.

"What was that?" asked Stanton.

"Skaskash playing with the mirrors," said Marian. "Probably the result of watching too many old movies." Cantrell's phone rang a couple of minutes later.

"Major Terry died at 1702," said Skaskash.

"I understand," said Cantrell. "Please send in Commander Lowell."

Lowell was waiting outside, crisply pressed, freshly shaved. He looked drawn, however, and there were lines in his face that hadn't been there a day or two before.

"Sit down, please, Commander," Cantrell said, indicating a chair beside his desk. "We are returning the NAUSS *Ciudad Juarez* to your command as of 1702 hours today."

"Unfortunately," added Marian, "we must detain some of your crew for further investigation." She handed him a copy of the ship's table of organization. "I have highlighted about a dozen names, all presently in custody."

"This is the political section and their informers," said Lowell.

"Oh, really?" said Marian. "In addition, we will provide you with a portion of the pretrial interrogation that may have a bearing on your forthcoming court-martial."

She touched a button, and the telecon screen lit up,

showing Major Terry and Commander Stanton being questioned by Dr. Yashon. Militia men stood in the background. Terry was explaining how he had placed the marines, and Dr. Yashon then asked: "Wasn't Captain Lowell supposed to keep a third of the marines on board ship?" Commander Stanton looked up and said: "That's *Commander* Lowell, and yes, he tried to overrule Major Terry's orders on that point. I told him the matter was political, and that since the ship was docked, I would take command if he didn't approve."

"That's a palpable forgery!" shouted Commander Stanton, struggling to his feet out of the deep, soft easy chair. "That's a damned lie! You're trying to save Lowell's ass by sticking it to *me*!"

"Major Terry also wrote a letter to Lowell saying essentially the same thing," said Marian.

"He didn't. He wouldn't. It's a forgery."

"He's right," said Lowell. "I never asked Major Terry what he was doing with the marines, and Stanton never threatened to take over the ship, even though he could have."

"You were remiss in your duty," Cantrell said, "but Terry is dead, and Stanton is going to be spending some time here on Rosinante, so my advice to you is to go home and lie like hell. You can pick up your CYA package on the way out."

"What does CYA mean?" asked Lowell.

"Cover Your Ass," replied Cantrell. "You expected to make captain without knowing that?"

Commander Lowell shrugged, and his face slipped into the poker-playing mode. "Thank you," he said. "I appreciate your effort on my behalf. If honor is lost, we can still lie enough to salvage the old career, can't we?"

"You *will* take the package, won't you?" Cantrell was startled and a little alarmed at honor appearing in a discussion about survival.

Commander Lowell nodded with a perfectly bland expression. "Of course," he said. "It gives me an option I hadn't considered."

After the meeting, Cantrell sat at his desk doodling triangles on a yellow pad. "I don't know," he said at last. "Maybe we should have kept the ship and negotiated for its release."

"No," said Marian. "What we want, the navy can't give,

and this way we cut the line between NAUGA-Navy and NAUGA-Security." She paused at the door. "More to the point, if the NAU refused to negotiate, we aren't strong enough to hold the ship."

# CHAPTER 27

On April 14, 2041, forty-one days after the Rosinante Incident, the Senate Security Committee met in closed session to hear the Administrator of NAUGA-Security, Dr. M. Stanley Bowman, testify on the continuation of the Panoblanquista movement despite the stern measures employed to repress it. In the afternoon session, Senator Gomez of Texas engaged in the following exchange.

Sen. G. Dr. Bowman, sir, this morning you identified the senior Panoblanquista agent remaining at large as C. Chavez Cantrell, presently the governor of Mundito Rosinante. What is he doing there to stir up trouble in Texas?

Dr. B. The Panoblanquistas are widespread, and have many interests. I expect Governor Cantrell is minding his own business until his time comes to act.

Sen. G. In other words, he isn't doing anything?

Dr. B. He resisted arrest. [laughter]

Sen. G. On what charges?

Dr. B. Suspicion of sedition, suspicion of treason, and conspiracy to aid and abet sedition. That was before March fourth, of course.

Sen. G. On what were the charges based?

Dr. B. We seized the files of Scadiwa, and a great deal of correspondence was from Mr. Cantrell. I'm not familiar with the details.

Sen. G. I am interested. Please have the details supporting the charges sent to my office by close of business tomorrow.

Dr. B. Of course, Senator.

Sen. G. According to our information, the fighting on Rosinante was precipitated by Lieutenant Holt's attempt to create a diversionary tactic by nuking the Prenatal Care Clinic. Did you approve of his choice of target?

Dr. B.   I had no advance knowledge—no, I didn't select the target, or authorize its selection.

Sen. G.   But do you approve of it, or condone its selection?

Dr. B.   I don't understand what you mean.

Sen. G.   You were one of the founders of the Creationist Coalition, were you not, Dr. Bowman?

Dr. B.   That was more than twenty years ago, Senator, and I have resigned from the organization long since.

Sen. G.   I understand. You resigned in the early thirties, did you not?

Dr. B.   In 2034. I could look up the exact date if you wish.

Sen. G.   What precipitated your resignation from the Creationist Coalition, Dr. Bowman?

Dr. B.   Basically, the refusal of the group to condemn lawless acts by a small number of extremists.

Sen. G.   That is commendable. Was the specific incident that led to your resignation a bombing, perhaps?

Dr. B.   Yes, I believe it was.

Sen. G.   Was it the bombing of the Rockefeller Institute in Cincinnati? You resigned less than a week afterward, according to the record.

Dr. B.   That may have been the incident, I don't remember.

Sen. G.   Please try to remember, Dr. Bowman. There is quite a lot of material suggesting that that bombing was indeed the incident that triggered your resignation.

Dr. B.   I remember. That *was* the incident, and the way the Coalition handled it provoked my resignation.

Sen. G.   Do you recall the name of the man who planted the bomb?

Dr. B.   No.

Sen. G.   The bombing is attributed to a man named Joe Bob Baroody. Do you know him?

Dr. B.   No, Senator, I do not.

Sen. G.   Might he not be one of the double agents that the MIS has used for various purposes?

Dr. B.   No, sir!

Sen. G.   You are aware that Lieutenant Holt had been identified as Baroody?

Dr. B.   Ah, ah—no. No. No, I hadn't heard that conjecture.

Sen. G.   It is not conjecture, Dr. Bowman, it is positive identification.

Dr. B.   That is an amazing coincidence, if true, Senator. Just amazing.

Sen. G.   Dr. Bowman, that isn't the half of it. The woman who died in the bombing was Dr. Susan Brown, as you may recall. The Prenatal Care Clinic on Rosinante —Lieutenant Holt's target—was operated by a computer from the Rockefeller Institute at Cincinnati. A computer designed and built by the colleagues of the late Susan Brown to continue the lines of work she had been pursuing at the time of her death. A computer known as Corporate Susan Brown, in fact! Do you stand by your claim that Holt/Baroody was not a double agent?

Dr. B.   Well, obviously it will have to be checked out. To my present knowledge he was not a double agent. I'll ask the commissioner about it.

Sen. G.   I shall ask him myself at tomorrow's session. He, also, is a member of the Creationist Coalition, is he not?

Dr. B.   I don't know. He used to be a member.

Sen. G.   There are a lot of Creationists in Security, aren't there, Mr. Administrator?

Dr. B.   Not so many, only a few percent—

Sen. G.   Six of your seven commissioners, and nineteen out of twenty-three assistant commissioners. Your closest associates. In fact, the prime target on Rosinante wasn't Cantrell at all, but Corporate Susan Brown, wasn't it?

Dr. B.   No. I don't know. I don't think so.

Sen. G.   Do you approve of Lieutenant Holt's choice of target for his so-called diversion, Dr. Bowman?

Dr. B.   Do you understand what issues were at stake, Senator Gomez?

Sen. G.   I understand that in the middle of an incipient civil war you and your Creationist henchmen saw fit to pursue a private vendetta against a dead woman. That you injure our friends, give comfort to our enemies, and waste lives and treasure trying to suppress an idea! Or perhaps Corporate Susan Brown is also a Panoblanquista?

Dr. B.   Alas, no. [laughter]

Sen. G.   Throwing good money after bad, you have also requested navy to provide a task force to remove Cantrell and other enemies of the NAU from Rosinante by force of arms. Is that correct?

Dr. B. We have made the request, but the navy is reluctant to go along with us. They say it would divert ships urgently needed in the L-four and L-five theaters.

Sen. G. They show better judgment than Security, at any rate. Certainly they show better judgment than you, Dr. Bowman. Have you given thought to resignation?

Maria Yellowknife picked up the hard copies from the tray.

"These are the columns and editorials on Tuesday's closed session," she said. "O'Donnell and Caldwell say you lower the boom on the administrator, but the rest are pretty cool. The *Phoenix Tribune* has an OpEd column by Jay Greiner headed 'Not Proven,' for instance."

Senator Gomez took the papers from his legislative assistant and leafed through them. "That's about what we expected. The evidence linking Bowman with the murder of Governor Panoblanco is entirely circumstantial," he said, "and don't forget that Bowman's supporters are willing to play dirty and rough."

"Right. To whom shall we leak today's closed session?"

"Let it sit a little," the senator said. "Instead, we can give O'Donnell and Caldwell the file on Joe Bob Baroody and let them ask why a terrorist killed trying to nuke a prenatal care clinic is being brought home for burial with full military honors. Then we start tying Joe Bob to NAUGA-Security and Stanley Bowman."

"Is that circumstantial also?" she asked.

"No." The senator opened a folder and removed a glossy photograph, the standard publicity shot of a politician shaking hands with one of his supporters, in this case, the mustached Dr. Bowman was shaking hands with a grinning Joe Bob in front of a banner that read "Baptists Against Darwin."

"Gonsalves also turned up a ninety-second film clip of Baroody warming up a crowd for someone he calls 'my good friend Stanlee Bowman,'" Gomez said. "That one I shall spring on 'St. Louis People' Friday a week."

The phone rang. Maria picked it up.

"Senator Gomez' office," she said.

"Office of the President," said a beautifully modulated female voice. "Mr. Robert Schlecter would like to arrange a teleconference with Senator Gomez." Bob Schlecter was the president's Chief of Staff.

"Schlecter would like a telecon meeting with you, Senator," said Maria.

"Fine," said Gomez. He walked over to the set, and sat down in his tall leather chair, flanked with the flags of the NAU and Texas. "Tell Bob I'm ready."

Schlecter appeared on the screen facing him after a tiny delay as the video signal was decoded, a big man, prematurely bald, wearing dark glasses.

"Good evening, Senator," he said genially. "You perhaps have an idea why I'm calling?"

"Bowman has offered to reisgn?" asked Gomez politely.

Schlecter laughed. "No. Bowman serves at the pleasure of the president. I wanted to congratulate you on the very effective presentation you made today. You did your homework and handed poor old Stanley his head on a silver platter." Maria Yellowknife took a little bow off camera as she left the room.

The senator smiled and fingered his mustache. "I thought he looked a little pained," he agreed.

"The fact is, the president is willing to unblock the funds for the Central Texas Desalinated Water project."

"That's nice, Bob. Central Texas could use the water. What about the Federal Judgeship for B.J. Coya?"

"The Panoblanquista?"

"The State Senator, Bob, *that* B.J. Coya."

"We'd have to dismiss the charges first."

"That wouldn't be hard, all things considered, would it now?"

"Look, Senator, I can promise to dismiss the charges. I can't promise the other, but I'll see what I can do."

"Of course, Bob. I know that. You'll do your best, just as always."

"In return, we'd like you to ease up on Bowman. You don't have to lay off—I imagine dumping on Security pulls pretty good in Texas—but ease up a little."

"Ease up enough, you mean?" Gomez smiled, showing his gold-capped bicuspid. "Give me one good reason, *por favor.*"

Schlecter sat back and looked thoughtful. "Okay, Senator. The NAU is in trouble with the Mexican Libre thing. Maybe you know that better than I do. The next year is going to be critical." The president was going to be up for reelection at the end of that year. "NAUGA-Security has been charged with holding the country together, and if you shoot down Administrator Bowman, most of the top staff will go with them."

"That would appear to be the case," agreed Gomez, "but none of them would be a—shall we say—tragic loss?"

"I can't think of any of them I really like," agreed Schlecter, "but as a group, it would be hard to replace them. NAUGA-Security would be dead in the water in the middle of a revolution."

"A revolution of water is a maelstrom," offered Gomez helpfully.

Schlecter looked puzzled, then laughed. "Block that metaphor!" he said. "But seriously, we can't afford to have NAUGA-Security down at a time like this."

"We can't afford to have dissident politicians blown up with cruise missiles, either," observed Gomez politely.

Schlecter shook his head. "Oh, hell, Senator, that's ancient history. Besides, there isn't any proof."

"And Governor Panoblanco got what was coming to him, right, Bob?"

"Don't put words in my mouth, Senator. He wasn't popular with the Administration, I'll be the first to admit it, but don't put words in my mouth."

"Of course, *amigo*. We will forget about poor Luis Raoul and his spectacular demise, but I find your reasons unpersuasive."

"Really?" Schlecter's face became impassive. "In what respect, please?"

Gomez had been about to say that the NAU was not a country, and that in the long run it could not be held together, but he thought the better of it.

"Do you really think that Stanley Bowman and his merry men are all that keeps the ship of state afloat in a sea of Chicano chicanery and Japanese gold?"

"Oh, hell no!" laughed Schlecter. "But we'd have a real dogfight confirming a new administrator if you shot him down. And Security is the mainstay against secession. It wouldn't do to screw it up in an election year, now, would it?"

"I can remember when Security was the mainstay against the old regime," said Gomez. "*Nobody* wanted *them* back. Times were simpler then."

"I suppose they were, Senator. Do we have a deal?"

"I will consider the matter," said Gomez after a moment's thought. "Perhaps it would help if the charges against B.J. Coya were dropped as an expression of the goodwill I am sure the president bears me."

Schlecter nodded. "Your office will receive word by midnight," he said, "and I will urge the president to approve Coya for the judgeship, for what that is worth."

If Schlecter strongly suspected that the answer was no, he didn't show it. The pretense of seeking an accommodation was itself a form of accommodation. The president's Chief of Staff looked at his watch. "Always a pleasure to do business with you, Senator," he said, and they each simultaneously reached out to break contact.

Six days later, on April 20, 2041, at 0405, the phone-secretary by Maria Yellowknife's bedside began to ring. After the third ring it began to ring louder. After the sixth ring, it turned on the lights. Maria sat up.

"Are you awake?" asked the phone.

"I am now," she said. "Who is it?"

"Corporate Zapata, the office manager."

"Well, put the call through," said Maria. "Whatever it is, I won't be sleeping any more tonight."

"Hello, Maria," said Corporate Zapata. "I regret to inform you that Senator Gomez' chartered plane undershot the runway at Abilene as it approached for landing, and crashed."

"What?"

"Senator Gomez died in the plane crash. The plane is still burning. It will not be known for a little while yet, but I was talking to him as the plane went down."

Maria tried to say: What, the senator dead? but all that came out was a tiny, choked-off wail. She sat on the bed looking at her folded hands, trying to practice her yoga breathing exercises and watching the tears run off the end of her nose.

"Senator Gomez left me contingency instructions," said Zapata, "and I need you here at the office immediately. I will request a police car to bring you over."

Maria pulled a tissue from the box and blew her nose. "Why?"

"I need you for the press conference," said Zapata. "I am unable to have a press conference without you or the senator present."

"I meant, why a police car?"

"For your own safety."

"Whatever you want," she said. The senator had a contingency plan, and she could for a little while act instead of thinking. "I'll dress right away."

There was a police car waiting in the driveway as she entered the lobby of her apartment building. She snapped open her purse phone, and hit the office button.

"Okay, Zapata. It is four thirty-two AM, and I am about to enter patrol car eight oh nine. Tell me about the contingency plan."

"Very good, Maria, you should be here by five ten or five fifteen and we can start to set up the press conference the senator wanted."

"The contingency plan is a press conference?" She entered the police car and identified herself.

"In part," said Zapata. "After Schlecter called, the senator suspected he might be in danger. He realized he could do little to protect himself, but he took steps to assure that if he should die, his message would be given maximum publicity." The police car rolled out of the driveway. "At his order, I used the question templates we have for the St. Louis press corp, and generated a dozen or so questions for each one based on the proposition 'What if the senator had just been killed?' He enjoyed answering them tremendously, and it was what he was doing when his plane went down. He said, if he was killed, we should take his recorded answers and have a press conference with the same reporters I had profiled for him. He thought that would be very funny."

"What good will it do?" Maria asked.

"It should bring confusion to his enemies," replied Zapata. "He is quite outspoken, and sometimes shows a total disregard for the laws of libel and slander. Also, it was his wish that it be done."

"Then we'll do it," said Maria, and snapped off the phone.

The death of Senator Gomez in a flaming plane crash was top-line news. The posthumous press conference was simply too good to pass up. The reporters lucky enough to be invited were at the senator's office despite lost sleep or missing breakfast. The conference began immediately on the heels of the 0700 news, which showed the plane crash in Abilene, and the senator's charred body being removed from the wreckage. Then, the announcer's voiceover:

"We interrupt our regular program to bring you 'live' from St. Louis a, ah, prerecorded press conference with the late Senator Gomez. Take it away, Fred."

The scene cut to Senator Gomez' office, showing the senator sitting in his tall-backed leather chair, with the flags of Texas and the NAU flanking him.

"Good morning," said the senator. "In the event that you see this broadcast, I will be dead. In the course of investigating NAUGA-Security, I came to realize that I might face death at the hands of agents of my own government. This now appears to be the case. First question, please."

"Roger Sims, Senator." Sims rarely functioned well until his second cup of coffee. "How will this affect your chances for reelection?" There was nervous laughter from the reporters.

"Let me say this," said the image of Senator Gomez. " 'If nominated I will not run. If elected, I will not serve.' I am, honest to God, really, truly dead." The last question before MIS plainclothesmen closed the news conference down forty-five minutes later was:

"Jane O'Donnell, Senator. Do you think Dr. Bowman of NAUGA-Security ordered you put to death?"

"I don't rightly know whether Bowman signed the order or not, but this here killing of Chicano politicians has just naturally got to stop!"

It was not rebroadcast domestically, but JapaNews picked it up and featured it, and the word, once out, stayed out.

The president's office was done in crystal and silver, with icy-blue accents and walls of pale, calm beige reflected in the mirrors and peer glasses set around the room. Bob Schlecter refilled his coffee cup from a pot on the serving tray beside him, and added cream and sugar.

"To be perfectly honest with you, Stan," he said, "I can't imagine how the president will be able to keep you on after that number Gomez did on you this morning."

"Lies, slanders, and half-truths," said Bowman. "The man is dead, but God damn his soul to hell for trying to push the country into a civil war!"

"I'm sorry, Stan," said Schlecter, setting his cup on the table beside him, "but to me it looked like Gomez was finally blowing the whistle on NAUGA-Security, as if he felt it was long overdue. I tried to get him off your case last week, you know, but he was sore about Governor Panoblanco, and wouldn't turn loose."

"He had no evidence. There *is* no evidence."

"Right. He admitted as much. Why was he so hell bent on making trouble, do you suppose?"

"He was a Panoblanquista."

"Senator Gomez? Not hardly. I think he meant it when he said: 'This here killing of Chicano politicians has just naturally got to stop.'" Schlecter took a sip of coffee. "He couldn't stick that to you, but he caught you riding your old antigenetic research hobby horse again, didn't he?"

"What if he did? The Fundamentalist-Creationist view is the by-God majority in this country," said Bowman.

"If you count the Chicanos, Messicans, and other Hispanics," agreed Schlecter. "But *they* are sore at you because of Panoblanco, Gomez, and company. And there are a lot of intellectuals with pointy heads who have been waiting to stick it to you for a long time." He shrugged. "Face it, Stan, you may be the issue that loses the president his reelection, even if he gives you the sack."

"Oh, hell, Bob—Security is the only thing holding this country together. The NAU will go to pieces without NAUGA-Security, and NAUGA-Security will be floundering around for years if you let the Chicanos pull me out of the driver's seat."

"That may possibly be the case," conceded Schlecter cautiously, "but if we don't do something about Security, you, personally, will be the issue that sinks the president. I swear it, Stan, you have got to go."

"Could we postpone the election?"

"Not bloody likely."

"Then the president has just got to choose between losing the election or letting the country disintegrate." Dr. M. Stanley Bowman sat back in his chair and wiped his glasses with an immaculately clean handkerchief. "History will not forgive a man who sacrifices his country to further his tawdry political aims."

"Perhaps." Schlecter set aside his empty cup. "However, you are not NAUGA-Security personified, whatever your aides may tell you, and the president may not see it your way. I tell you quite frankly, *I* don't. His best bet has got to be accepting your resignation and counting on inertia to hold the country together. I don't think the NAU is in so much trouble that it will vanish in a puff of smoke if the president gives you the sack."

"I'm not NAUGA-Security," agreed Bowman, "but you can't blow the head off an agency in the middle of a crisis and expect it to go on functioning smoothly. In this case, I expect it wouldn't function at all. And don't forget, Bob, there are other problems beside Mexico Libre, such as—" His belt phone rang, and he snapped it open. "What is it?" he barked. "I'm in a very important conference." There was a pause. "It's Deputy Administrator Hulvey," he told Schlecter. "Can we put him on the telecon?"

"It's *your* job termination interview, Stan. Put him on if you want."

Bowman fussed around with his phone for a moment, and the deputy administrator appeared in the peer glass by their seats, sitting behind a massive mahogany desk with the carven and polychromed seal of NAUGA-Security on the front. He looked at Schlecter, and shrugged.

"We have a mutiny in the fleet," he said flatly. "The first reports are just coming in. It looks bad."

"I am a political liability," said Bowman, folding his hands over his vested paunch, and looking at Schlecter over his glasses. "Ask your own damn questions."

"What happened?" asked the president's Chief of Staff.

"The senior officers in the L-five Fleet are caucussing, and the political officers—the ones we can reach—are talking about 'limiting the damage,' " he said.

Bowman forgot about being a political liability. "Goddamn them! They have the responsibility to prevent this shit! They have the authority to stop it! Tell them to start making arrests!"

"That didn't work in the L-four Fleet," said Hulvey. "We lost a lot of people trying. We took control of the NAUSS *Vancouver* and the NAUSS *Phoenix*, but we have lost contact with both ships."

"What do you mean, 'lost contact'?" asked Bowman.

"We are out of audio contact with both ships," Hulvey replied, "and the *Phoenix* does not show on the radar screens of any stations still responsive to our command." His desk pushed a paper at him. "Laputa radar reports that the *Vancouver* faded off the screen at fifteen thirty-four—about a minute ago." He covered his eyes with one hand. "My son Dave was the political officer on the *Vancouver*," he whispered. His desk pushed another paper at him, and he took it. "The Fourth Marine Division is preparing to embark on shuttles for Laputa. They will be ready to take off by twenty-four hundred hours at the latest and they need flight clearance before then"—he did a laugh very hard, and got hold of himself with an effort. "Excuse me. The ozone layer isn't a laughing matter, is it? It's just that we haven't had any sunspots, latey—lately—so we can't send up the Ma—Ma—" He dissolved in laughter.

"I'll talk to Bannerman right away," said Schlecter. "That waiver has got to be expedited!"

"Don't bother, Bob," said the president. "I'm going to declare martial law." He had been watching Bowman's dismissal, and had made an unobtrusive entrance. Schlecter and Bowman stood up, and so, laughing helplessly, did MIS Deputy Administrator Hulvey.

"Sir," said Bowman urgently, "this is Senator Gomez' fault. And the fault of the networks for broadcasting his slanderous and seditious raving—"

"BOWMAN!" screamed the president. "You bloody-handed idiot! You traitorous fucking fool! *You* did it! Guards! GUARDS!" Several plainclothes officers ran into the room. "Take this son of a bitch out and shoot him." They hesitated.

"You heard me," said the president. "What's the matter?"

"You have to declare martial law first, sir," said his Chief of Staff. He opened a concealed cabinet and spoke to a computer terminal. It pushed up a piece of paper, and Schlecter laid it on the sensing plate.

"You sign, I witness, and it is done, sir," he said. "Are you sure this is the way to go?"

The president read the paper and signed it on the sensing plate. "There is no longer any choice in the matter," he said. Then he turned to the guards. "The command is legal." They seized Dr. M. Stanley Bowman and hustled him out of the room. A single shot was heard from the atrium.

"So much for Mortimer," said the president. "Now then, Hulvey. When did this trouble in the fleet start?"

"About oh nine hundred today, sir," replied Hulvey, no longer laughing.

"It might have been the Gomez press conference," said a shaken Schlecter.

"That probably helped," Hulvey agreed, "but it was the NAUSS *Ciudad Juarez* under Commander Lowell that set things off. He rendezvoused with the L-four Fleet and broadcast a fire-eating speech calling for the restoration of the Old Regime and a Free Mexico. And he finished by playing 'Guantanomera' and 'The Star Spangled Banner.' "

"I see," said the president. "Well, get the marines up to Laputa. The sooner, the better."

"Won't that cut the grain harvest this fall?" asked Schlecter.

"This fall?" asked the president. "We'll be lucky to make it to the end of the week."

# CHAPTER 28

Commander McInterff entered Cantrell's office in his best dress uniform.

"I've been chatting up such of the NAUGA-Navy chaps as haven't gone over to the Old Regime," he said, "and it's very strange they would have me running back and forth rather than talking to yourself direct."

"Protocol," said Marian. "They had you acting as their ambassador."

"Really?" asked McInterff. "And can it be put in my job description?"

"It might be worth another stripe someday," she said.

"What did they say?" asked Cantrell.

"They agreed to your terms, mainly," replied McInterff. He opened his briefcase and handed Marian some papers. "See for yourself."

She looked through them unhurriedly.

"They do indeed," she said. "Someone named Schlecter confirms you as governor of Rosinante, and NAUGA-Security lists the charges against you—which are pretty damn trivial, by the way—and drops them with prejudice. Is Hulvey heading up Security now?"

"Acting head," said Skaskash. "There are reports that Bowman was shot, but we can't get confirmation."

"Don't you think you might do better staying neutral, sir?" asked McInterff. "The NAU is coming apart at the seams, and you could be in serious deep trouble if the other side wins."

"We'd have to take sides sooner or later," said Cantrell, "and this way we get credit for volunteering."

"Maybe so," agreed McInterff doubtfully, "but do you really think you made the right choice?"

"That's a good question," said Marian. "The best you

can say is that it has to be better to make the wrong choice immediately than to temporize and stall until you no longer have the choice to make."

"You don't sound terribly eager to administer my loyalty oath," said Cantrell.

"To be frank, I had hoped you would stand for the Old Regime, sir."

"I should have rather done so," replied Cantrell, "but this way is better for Rosinante."

"I'm almost done with the preamble," said Skaskash. "When the red light goes on, you will be broadcast live all over the Solar System."

Blink.

"At this time, and in this place, do you, Charles Chavez Cantrell, swear to support the North American Union against all enemies, foreign and domestic?" asked McInterff.

"I do," replied Cantrell firmly.

"And on the next day, and for all time hence, do you still so swear?"

"I do."

"Then the president of the NAU proclaims you his governor of Rosinante, under the laws of the NAU and of Rosinante," said McInterff. "Repeat after me: I do solemnly swear that I will faithfully execute the office of Governor of Rosinante . . ." Cantrell repeated it. " . . . and will to the best of my ability, preserve, protect and defend the Constitution of the United—of Rosinante."

Cantrell repeated it without the stumble.

Blink.

"*That* should set some teeth on edge," said Skaskash. "Maybe you won't be getting that extra stripe after all, Commander."

"Pity," said Commander McInterff with a faint smile.

Outside the band struck up "Dixie."

"They sound a lot better with the Union trumpeters," said Cantrell.

"When they start to play 'The Impossible Dream' you go out on the reviewing stand," Skaskash reminded them. "Then we have the speech, and the parade, and the party. The autobuffets are already in place."

"Not another three-day party," said Cantrell. "I don't think I'd be up to it."

"Oh, of course not," said Skaskash, "there are too many

families with small children for that. No, this time we party and picnic and play games until we round out the evening with fireworks."

"Where did we get fireworks on such short notice?" asked Cantrell.

"Mordecai Rubenstein has the most remarkable recipe book," said Marian, "and when I told him how much I enjoyed fireworks . . . why, he practically thrust them upon me." She smiled. "We have a twenty-five-minute display. I think he would have had his machines make more, except that we began to worry about having to wash the purlin window."

When Cantrell walked out on the balcony, he couldn't hear whether the band was playing or not. He raised his arms above his head to acknowledge the cheering of his people.

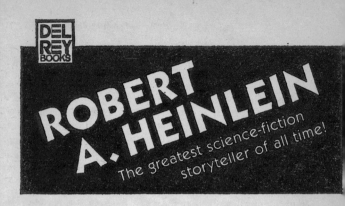